Lydia has made her decision.

With growing conviction that she knew what she wanted and where she wanted to be, she headed for the door and threw it open. Only one thing would change her mind. And that was up to Reverend Law.

He looked up as she stood in the doorway. "Are you ready?"

Lydia faced him squarely. "I've decided I'm not going." She met his eyes without blinking. If he had any interest in her as a woman, this was the time to proclaim it.

His mouth dropped and he gathered himself up. "You've what?"

"I've decided I'm not going. At least not to the Laartz's." Would he understand her meaning? She waited. *Give me a better offer and I'll jump at the chance.* But he simply stared at her.

"Lydia, you can't be serious. You're alone here with two unmarried men. Think how it looks. Your reputation will be ruined."

"I'm very serious. Besides, you keep forgetting Granny." She stiffened her spine. Perhaps she had imagined his kindly interest meant more than it did. "I have a pleasant home here and I have a job to do. I'm going to stay and do it."

"Lydia, you're making a big mistake."

"I'm sorry you came all the way out here for nothing, but I'm not leaving." She blinked hard, determined her eyes would not glisten with tears. If only he would say something that gave her reason to hope he had plans for the future.

LINDA FORD draws on her own experiences living in the Canadian prairie and Rockies to paint wonderful adventures in romance and faith. She lives in Alberta, Canada, with her family, writing as much as her full-time job of taking care of a paraplegic and four kids who are still at home will allow. Linda says, "I thank God that He has given me a full, productive life and that I'm not bored. I thank Him for placing a little bit of the creative energy revealed in His creation into me, and I pray I might use my writing for His honor and glory."

Books by Linda Ford

HEARTSONG PRESENTS
HP240—The Sun Still Shines
HP268—Unchained Hearts

The Heart Seeks a Home

Linda Ford

Heartsong Presents

Dedicated to my sister, Leona, who listens to me talk about the people in my books as if they are real, who accompanies me on research trips, and into used book stores; and to my sister-in-law, Shawna, who listens to me talk about my stories, provides kind and constructive feedback, and shares my love of writing. They say you can pick your friends but not your relatives. For both of you, if it had been up to me to choose, I couldn't have picked anyone better. Thanks.

A note from the author:
I love to hear from my readers! You may correspond with me by writing:
Linda Ford
Author Relations
PO Box 719
Uhrichsville, OH 44683

ISBN 1-57748-754-0

THE HEART SEEKS A HOME

Cover illustration by Victoria Lisi and Julius.

PRINTED IN THE U.S.A.

one

April 1914 in Alberta, Canada

She should have known better. The instant she saw them lounging at the edge of the railway platform and studying her from under wide-brimmed cowboy hats she should have been warned. Certainly when they ambled over to ask if she was Miss Lydia Baxter, and their startled looks when she said she was, should have given her cause for concern. When they announced they were to take her to the Twin Spurs Ranch, she should have grabbed her valise and stepped back on the train.

But now it was too late.

"There must be some mistake," she murmured, her voice catching deep in her throat. Mistake! If what they said was true, the word didn't begin to address the magnitude of her situation.

Quivers raced up and down her body. If she didn't sit down right now she was going to fall on her face. Her distress must have been evident to the two men, for one of them—the shorter, heavier one who had introduced himself as—but she couldn't recall his name—grabbed a chair and shoved it under her. She sank into it, her limbs shaking like straws in the wind, her face burning hot then, seconds later, cold and clammy.

"I'm sorry. I can't stay. You'll have to take me back." Her teeth rattled as she talked, and she gripped her hands in her lap to slow their shaking.

The men exchanged looks. The taller one shuffled his feet and looked around the room. The other leaned back against the door twisting his hat in his hands.

"Y–you must ta–take me back to town. I–I can't possibly stay here." She prayed they would not see how frightened she

5

was. "I thought I was going to work for a family."

"A nice family for you," Reverend Williams had said. "You'll have a good home."

Suspicion burned at the back of her mind. Had he knowingly sent her to this situation? Immediately she dashed the thought away. It wasn't possible. He and Mrs. Williams would be as shocked as she to discover there was no family, only two young bachelors who steadfastly refused to look at her or respond to her demands to be taken back to town so she could get back on the train and go—

Go where? She had no place to go.

It didn't matter. Anyplace was better than this.

She cleared her throat. Two pairs of eyes flicked toward her. "Did you hear me?" she demanded in stronger tones. "You must take me back."

The one at the door straightened. "Well now, I don't rightly see how we can. You can see it's already dark out. And no trains run tonight. Guess you'll have to stay."

Lydia stared at him long and hard. Matt Weber. That's what he'd called himself when he sauntered up to her at the train station and hoisted her trunk on his shoulder with an ease that made her gasp. His brown mustache twitched under her scrutiny.

The other man stepped forward, and Lydia shifted her gaze to him. His name returned as well. Sam Hatten. Taller and slighter, his blue eyes met hers for a moment, then he looked away, rubbing a hand over his thatch of blond hair.

"I'm sorry, Ma'am," he said. "This really is as much a surprise to us as to you." He cleared his throat. "We were expecting a spinster, not. . ." His gaze darted to her face and then past her shoulder. "But we decided we might as well make the best of a bad situation. Besides, it really is too far to go back to town now, and it is, as Matt says, already dark."

She shrank inward and hugged her arms around her. This was the worst situation she'd ever been in. There was no one in these hills to come to her rescue.

Matt jammed his hat on his head. "I'm going to put the horses away." And he fled out the door.

Sam turned and lifted the stove lid to stir the fire. "I think we should have tea," he mumbled.

Lydia couldn't breathe. Her heart thudded so loudly she was sure it drowned out the noise of Sam dipping water and pouring it into the kettle. She stared at his back as he stood over the stove waiting for the kettle to boil and then poured the hot water over the tea leaves in a squat brown teapot.

She couldn't think what she should do. These men were certainly not prepared to take her back to town. She studied the door but it didn't make sense for her to walk out into the dark. A shudder raced across her shoulders. From what she'd seen as they drove up to the house in the dusk it would be worth her life and limb to wander around these hills in the dark. And heaven knows what sort of wild animals would share the night. She shivered and looked again at Sam's back. Animals outside; two men in. What was the difference?

Sam set a teacup in front of her and filled it. He poured himself a cupful, sitting opposite her. Still not speaking, he added two spoonfuls of sugar.

The door rattled open and Lydia jumped.

Matt entered, grabbed a cup, and joined them at the table.

Sam stirred his tea and sighed. He looked long and hard at Matt then turned to Lydia. "I'm sorry, but I think you really will have to stay." He sipped his tea. "No doubt things will look better in the morning." Suddenly he rose to his feet. "I'll take your things to your room, and you can make yourself comfortable." He scooped up her bag and headed to the doorway of the next room.

She gulped her tea and lurched to her feet, hesitating as she struggled to think what she should do. Stay? Go? Sit? Follow her bag?

Her bag and the small trunk on the wagon contained all that remained of her life, so she hurried after Sam.

He stepped into a dark room.

She hung back while he lit a lamp then turned to leave, pausing at her side to look down and say, "You'll be perfectly safe, you know." He waited for her to step into the room then pulled the door closed as he left.

She stared after him. Safe? Hardly! There wasn't a place in the world where she could feel safe. For a while she thought she'd found a place with the Williamses. But that, too, had come to an end.

She dropped to the edge of the bed and hunched over her knees.

Oh, Mother, if only you hadn't left me I wouldn't be at the mercy of others. Thinking of her mother brought a measure of calm.

A great weariness overcame her, but she commanded her leaden limbs to move. The first thing she must do was secure the room.

She checked the door, but there was no lock or key.

A straight-backed chair sat in the shadows by a desk and she carried it to the door and shoved it firmly under the knob. It wouldn't stop much but would at least warn her if someone tried to intrude.

With arms that seemed too weak to function, she opened her bag and removed her brush. She pulled the hairpins out and let her hair fall loose down her back, brushing it with little care then braiding it into one thick plait for the night. Her thoughts unraveled as she twisted the braid.

Was it only this morning she had said good-bye to Reverend and Mrs. Williams and kissed the children?

How could they have sent her to this place?

She had trusted them when they brought her with them from England to Canada, promising she would always have a home with them. A bitter taste rose in her throat. A promise easily forgotten after two short years when Mrs. Williams' niece, Annabelle, wrote asking if she could stay with them. It was clear she was a hired servant easily disposed of.

She choked back tears. As she returned the brush to her bag

her hand touched her Bible and she brought it out, tenderly stroking its soft cover. At the end of a day Mother would sit in her rocker and no matter how weary, she'd read a chapter to Lydia.

"Lydia," she'd say in her gentle voice, "I want you to remember, God is faithful. He cares for you in a special way. He will never leave you nor forsake you."

It had been easy to believe those words while Mother was alive. Lydia shuddered, remembering some of the unwelcome surprises the world had offered a young girl alone in the world.

She looked at the Bible on her lap. "You were wrong, Mother," she whispered. "God doesn't care about me. No one does."

With trembling hands and aching heart, she pushed the Bible back into the valise and, without removing her clothes, crawled into bed. For a moment she thought about leaving the lamp on then sighed and turned it down until it died. Her eyes felt too large for her face as she stared into darkness that reached past the walls of this room into her future and down to her inmost being. She lay tense and wide-eyed as the night deepened, afraid to shut her eyes in case. . .in case. . .

ঽ৯

Light glared through a large square window. Lydia blinked and shot up to a sitting position. She hadn't expected to sleep so soundly nor to meet the morning unharmed.

Beyond the walls of the room muted noises warned her there were still two men in the house. Boot-clad feet thudded across the floor sending echoes of dread into the pit of her stomach. The sulfur smell of a match was followed by the pungency of wood chips burning. The aroma of coffee called her to get up.

Instead, Lydia lay down and drew the covers up to her neck. Bits of conversation drifted to her.

". . .can't keep her. . ."

". . .until something else. . ."

". . .misunderstanding. . ."

She was sure the soft voice belonged to Sam, the blue-eyed one, and the deeper voice to Matt, the stockier one.

A knock at her door sent her scurrying deeper under the covers. She lifted her head enough to see the chair still hooked under the knob then lay in a quivering huddle.

"Miss Baxter? Lydia Baxter? Are you there?" It was Matt outside her door. A louder knock and another call. "Lydia Baxter?" Then a call to the other one. "She's still in there, isn't she?"

Sam's voice joined Matt's. "Miss Baxter? Are you in there?"

Her eyes widened as they rattled the knob and she clutched the covers to her chin. Any minute they would break down the door.

"If you're there, please answer."

They wouldn't hear if she screamed. Nobody would.

Suddenly the chair jumped and Lydia screeched. The door opened a crack and two heads appeared in the space. She shrank back, her hands knotted along the top of the quilt.

Matt chuckled. "I see you're all right. Breakfast will be ready in a few minutes." He ducked out of sight.

Sam hesitated for a heartbeat then, letting his breath out in a whoosh, silently followed his partner.

Lydia waited for her trembling to pass then swung her weak legs over the side of the bed and reached for her bag. Her hand touched the Bible where she had shoved it last night, and she jerked it out. It fell open to the bookmark. Mother's words came to her.

Read a few verses every day then pray about your day, expecting and trusting God to guide you.

Lydia's hand hovered over the pages, but it was a habit too old to ignore. And somehow to do other than Mother had instructed made Lydia feel guilty, so she read Psalm 54, the reading for the day. The words so perfectly fit the ache in her heart that she bent closer and read them again. "Save me. . . hear my prayer. . .strangers are risen up against me. . .God is mine helper. . .he hath delivered me out of all trouble."

She closed her eyes and breathed the words deep into her soul then whispered a prayer for God's help and intervention.

Only then did she return the Bible to her bag and pull out the pink and blue printed shirtwaist. It was dreadfully wrinkled, but she shrugged out of the soiled and equally wrinkled white one she'd slept in and pulled on the clean. Freeing her hair from its braid, she brushed it quickly, with little regard for the results. Not bothering to check for a mirror, she simply twisted her hair into a knot at the back of her neck and pinned it in place.

At the door she took a long, shaky breath. She must convince these men to take her back to town. Immediately. She lifted her chin and stepped into the kitchen. In order to keep her hands from trembling, she clasped them together at her waist.

Matt sprang to his feet. "Here, have a chair." He pulled one from the table then straddled his own, arms resting on the runged back.

"How about some coffee?" Sam held a steaming cup toward her.

"Thank you," Lydia whispered, welcoming the warmth as she clutched the cup in cold hands.

"Well now," Matt began. "Let's talk about your job."

Lydia cleared her throat. "Excuse me." It was barely a whisper and she tried again. "Excuse me. This really is impossible. You must take me back. I thought I was going to work for a family. Not for two—" Her voice faded again. "Bachelors."

Matt looked at her with narrowed eyes. "We understand that. And you can bet we were equally surprised."

His unblinking stare made Lydia duck her head. He continued. "Where were you planning to go?"

She jerked her head up and met his unwavering brown eyes. "I. . .it's. . .there. . ."

"Do you have a place to go? Family in this country?" His dark eyes probed for answers.

Mutely, she shook her head.

"What about money? You got enough to get you someplace and take care of yourself until you find something?" Again that probing, prodding look.

She thought of the twenty dollars Reverend Williams had given her as a farewell gift and wondered how far that would take her.

Sam leaned over the table and fixed her with his blue eyes. "You see we're finding we have too much work to do outside to look after things in the house."

Her gaze swept around the room and she knew at a glance that he spoke the truth. The whole room was littered several feet high and wore a grimy coat.

Sam smiled acknowledgment of her silent assessment. "So this is what we have in mind. You stay here and work." He leaned back and before she could answer, added, "We'll pay you well, and when you find another place or a job you think is as good as here, we'll take you there immediately. Deal?"

Matt leaned forward on his arms, a lazy expression on his face, but Lydia guessed he was waiting for her answer as anxiously as Sam, who tipped his chair back and kept his eyes on her.

"Seems to me it would help us all out." Matt's low drawl filled the silence as Lydia stared from one man to the other.

"What will people think?" Lydia blurted out the thing uppermost in her mind.

Matt sat up, a scowl drawing his brows together. "I do not think right and wrong are determined by what people think or even what they say."

She shrank back from the anger in his voice.

"If people want to find something awful to say then they will whether or not you or I give them cause." He jerked to his feet and rubbed his thick black hair into a mass of curls.

Lydia glanced nervously at Sam, but he rose and went to the stove to stir the porridge, seemingly unaffected by Matt's reaction.

Matt rested a foot on his chair and turned to face her, a half smile on his face. "The way I see it is we need a housekeeper. And you need a place to stay."

Lydia stared at Sam's back and again at Matt's crooked smile. She certainly needed a place to stay, but Matt's words were only partly correct. It sometimes mattered a great deal what people thought. And she didn't need a third opinion to know it was wrong to live here alone with two men.

Matt nodded, taking her silence for consent, but from someplace deep inside her, Lydia discovered an inner strength that surprised her. She pulled herself straight in the chair and pushed her back against the hard rungs. "I'm sorry," she whispered. "I understand your predicament and I'd like to help out." Her voice grew stronger with each word. "But I cannot stay here under these circumstances"—She threw her hands in the air—"without some sort of chaperon."

Sam turned and stared at her.

Matt dropped his foot to the floor with a resounding thud that jarred up Lydia's spine, but she did not shrink back or lower her gaze. These men must understand that she would not allow herself to be put in such a situation.

Sam turned and filled bowls with steaming porridge and carried them to the table along with a pitcher of milk. Lydia's mouth watered when she saw the thick layer of yellowish cream floating on top of the milk. It was breakfast-time yesterday that she had last eaten, and suddenly nothing seemed as important as food. She pulled a bowl close.

"Help yourself." Sam pushed the cream and brown sugar close. Matt spun his chair around and sat down.

Lydia paused, glancing from one man to the other. From that same unprobed strength, she smiled, and keeping her voice soft, said, "Perhaps someone should give thanks first."

Matt's eyes narrowed. Sam practically jolted in his seat. Silence hung over the table. Finally, Sam cleared his throat and mumbled, "Go ahead."

She nodded and bowed her head, murmuring a short, simple

prayer. "Amen." She reached for the pitcher and poured a generous amount of cream into her bowl. There was sweet comfort in the warm, rich food, and for a moment Lydia forgot her predicament.

Sam pushed aside his empty bowl and stared into his coffee cup. Suddenly, he slapped the table with his open palm, almost causing Lydia to jump from her chair. "I got it!" he shouted. "Granny Arness!"

Matt glowered at him. "What about Granny Arness?"

"I was talking to Eldon Reimer in town awhile back, and he said something about not needing her anymore but there didn't seem to be anyplace for her." He shrugged. "Don't rightly remember all he said. I wasn't paying much attention."

Matt sat back, his face thoughtful. "It just might work."

Lydia leaned forward. "Who is Granny Arness?"

They both spoke at once. "She's—" Matt sat back and waited for Sam to explain. "Granny is a widow with no home of her own. She helps out at different places." He grinned smugly.

"If she could come here. . ." Matt nodded. "Sam, I think you've hit on a good idea."

Two pairs of eyes regarded Lydia. She studied the tabletop, running her fingernail along a crack in the wood. Despite the prospect of a chaperon, her mind was still troubled.

She slowly raised her head, looking at Sam first. "I still don't know anything about either of you." She turned from blue eyes to brown. "Apart from your names."

Matt's expression hardened a moment then he smiled, the change making him seem suddenly younger and not so formidable. "Fair enough. I'm more than twenty-five and less than thirty."

Sam snorted. "Who you trying to kid? I'm guessing if you're less than thirty, it's only by a sliver."

Matt cocked his head. "A very large sliver if you must know." He pushed back from the table and, tipping his chair back, hooked the heel of his boot over the bottom rung. "I'm not married. Never have been. I've never been in trouble with the law. I pay my bills on time and that's about it." His gaze moved to Sam.

Sam nodded. "I'm twenty-three this summer. Haven't had time to get married. Running this ranch leaves time for little else."

Matt nodded.

Lydia gave the crack in the table her full attention. Neither of them had mentioned God or church or family. A dark and familiar feeling hovered at the edges of her mind. She recognized it from the past. The sense of having little choice in the direction of her life. She sighed and the shadow receded. At least she'd gained one victory. Granny Arness.

Matt broke the silence. "Let's make a deal. We'll get Granny Arness to come. You help us for a few days—say until we get the cows moved to spring pasture—and then we'll discuss it again."

They took her silence for consent and pushed back from the table. Sam donned a worn denim coat. "I'll get the wagon ready."

Matt nodded. "I'll empty out the little room and put up a bed."

"Wait." Lydia squeaked, but Matt had already disappeared into the doorway next to the kitchen.

Sam turned at her call. "You'll do okay," he said before he left.

For several seconds she stared at the closed door then clamped her teeth tight. It seemed there was no choice but to stay. She was trying to trust God to take care of her, but sometimes it was hard to see how He was doing it.

She unclenched her jaw and rose to do the dishes.

Matt came through the room, struggling under a load of crates and lengths of leather. "I've uncovered the cot. I'll store this stuff in the barn."

She waited until the door closed behind him before she turned and gave the room a sweeping gaze then looked beyond to the far room. If she were to be stuck in this place she would at least have a good look at it.

Three doors stood along the wall of the far room. The first was the room for Granny Arness. Lydia peeked in. It was a narrow room with a cot on one side. The long, narrow window looked out over the green hillside.

The far door she guessed to be the men's bedroom, and she averted her eyes and retraced her steps to the middle one, stepping into the room where she'd spent the night. A glance revealed a desk and chair beneath the window, the tousled bed, and narrow wardrobe. She stooped and smoothed the covers then turned to face the front room which was slightly less messy than the kitchen. The oiled logs of the wall held a surprising array of objects.

She circled the room to better see the mounted deer heads, deer horns sporting a variety of hats, a rifle hanging across two hooks, and on a nail, a gun belt with the initials MW. She paused before a series of pictures mounted in plain black frames. One was of a man and woman standing beside a stately brick house. The next showed a young man in a school uniform holding a parchment in his hands. She leaned closer. The boy held a definite resemblance to Sam.

With brisk steps she moved to the other side of the room. Light bathed her as she stood in an alcove encircled by windows. Even the door contained a long window. She closed her eyes, letting warmth flood her, then stepped forward for a better look, gasping as a wave of dizziness swept through her. The house was set on a couch of green grass that dipped and rolled until it came to a white-ringed lake far below. The distance had laundered the greens to a smoky gray.

Her head swam as she stared. She grasped the window frame to steady herself but could not tear her eyes from the scene. Something stirred in her. A nameless feeling. A sense of discovery. Of being uncovered. It was not altogether an unwelcome sensation mounting inside and calling to her.

Lydia tore herself away and hurried back to the kitchen

where she looked about in dismay. Piles of neglected belongings filled every corner and swarmed over every surface. She wrinkled her nose and identified the brown puddles under the coats as the source of the pungent aroma.

Fresh panic assailed her.

How was she to bring order to this chaos?

Where did she begin?

She sank into a chair. She knew how to clean and how to cook a few simple things, but that was all. A smile tipped the corners of her mouth. It was what they deserved—an inexperienced housekeeper. She sniffed. She'd never been in charge before, but on the other hand, she'd never seen such a mess either.

A quick inspection of the cupboards revealed the cleaning supplies she needed, and she tackled the smelly corner, throwing the boots and coats out of the way. The smell was enough to make her eyes water. She was on her knees, head-first in the corner, when the door opened. Lydia sat back on her heels, feeling trapped. She blinked at the pair of legs that moved toward her.

"Well now, what are you doing sitting on the floor?" Matt asked. He dropped something on the table and hunched down beside her. "I didn't mean to startle you," he said, his voice deep. He waited and watched.

Lydia swallowed three times and blinked her eyes.

"Here, let me help you up." He rose and offered his hand. She looked at it, big and strong, then gingerly reached up and allowed him to pull her to her feet. "You're sure a timid young thing," he said as she pulled her hand away.

Her cheeks warmed.

Matt turned to the table. "I thought you might need some meat for dinner so I brought in some pork."

She looked at the raw slab of flesh on the table. It didn't look like anything she was familiar with. Did she fry it, roast it, or boil it? At Matt's sudden shout of laughter, she looked up.

"Do you know how to cook this?"

The corners of her mouth drooped. "I'm afraid not."

"Do you know how to cook anything?"

"One or two things." The Williamses had always had a cook.

He laughed again. "Well, don't that beat all. We've looked for a housekeeper for months. Some refused to live so far from town. One had a passel of young 'uns. Another had a dog she had to bring. There was one sounded pretty good, then she sent a letter full of 'house rules' as she called them. No smoking. No drinking. No swearing." He snorted and rolled his eyes. "She had more rules than most mothers. We finally get some-one to come here and it turns out you don't want to be here. On top of that, you can't cook. If that don't beat all." He laughed. "Well now. I guess I came along just in time to give you a cooking lesson."

He pulled out a bin to reveal a mixture of vegetables. He strode back and forth showing her where to locate flour, pans, salt, sugar, and more. He sliced the meat for frying, measured flour and lard for biscuits, and then scooped up his hat.

"Do you think you can manage?"

She drew a deep breath and glanced around the kitchen try-ing to recall all the instructions he had rattled off. She looked at him with a sense of awe. "How did you learn to cook?"

He chuckled in deep rolling bursts. "I've been on my own a long time. It was a matter of survival."

She smiled shyly. "Thank you for helping."

"Sam's gone for Granny Arness, and I'm headed to check the far fence line." He backed from the room. "I expect it will be almost suppertime before either of us are back." He paused. "You'll do fine." The door closed behind him.

Lydia smiled. He'd been so kind and helpful. She hummed as she returned to cleaning the corner.

two

She worked steadily all afternoon, finding a soothing calmness in the physical effort. So intent was she on her work that the sound of a wagon rattling to the door made her jerk up in surprise.

Sam stepped through the door bearing a wooden rocker in his arms. "Wait there," he called over his shoulder. "I'll be right back to give you a hand."

He set the chair to one side then went back, his voice coming to Lydia. "Here now." And then, "Take my arm."

Lydia stared at the door waiting for her first glimpse of Granny Arness. Sam returned, his steps measured and slow, a small woman clutching his arm. Lydia's first impression was of a rounded back and coarse gray hair bundled into an untidy bun.

Her mouth hanging open, Lydia stared. She didn't know what she had expected but certainly not this frail, half-crippled person who with Sam's help hobbled to the rocker, groaning as she eased herself into it. Any thought of a bustling, kindly, helpful sort of mother-figure immediately vanished.

Aware of Sam's scrutiny, she jerked her mouth shut and met his eyes. He shrugged then bent over the woman. "Granny, this is Lydia Baxter, the girl I—"

Granny waved a hand. "I know who she is." Her voice rasped.

Lydia blinked. The sharp tone could be from pain, for she was sure every move the older lady made must hurt, or—trepidation rushed to her heart—it could be irritability.

"You can call me Granny. Sam here said he was in need of a chaperon." Granny sniffed, leaving Lydia no doubt how she

19

felt about the living arrangements. "I explained to Sam my rheumatism has gotten so bad this past winter I can't do much work." She groaned again.

Sam edged toward the door. "I'll bring in your bags."

Granny nodded, her faded blue eyes studying Lydia. "Child, could you get me some tea?"

"Of course." Lydia sprang to do as she was bid.

A few minutes later she handed Granny a steaming cup. Something had been bothering her since Granny hobbled through the door, and she rested her hands on the arm of the chair. "I'm sorry to be adding to your discomfort."

Granny's gnarled fingers clasped Lydia's hand. "Don't be thinking any of this is your fault, child. I've been in pain most of the winter." She clucked her tongue. "The wagon ride didn't help, but I'll get over that soon enough." She patted Lydia's hand. "I'm afraid I'll be more trouble than I'm worth. I have so many poor days."

Lydia blinked back a sudden sting in her eyes. Granny was homeless, too—depending on the wants and charity of others for a roof over her head. Right there and then, Lydia promised herself that no matter what, she would do all she could to make Granny comfortable.

Sam came through with a small trunk which he carried to Granny's room. He stepped back into the kitchen; his gaze rested on Granny a moment, then he sought Lydia's eyes. "Will supper be ready in an hour or so?"

Lydia nodded, stilling the panic at trying to remember what Matt had told her. She studied the top of Granny's head knowing she would benefit from the older woman's experience. But Granny handed her the empty cup and said, "I'd dearly love to stretch out for a few minutes."

"Of course." Lydia sprang toward the door. "I'll make the bed."

"Thank you, my dear. I brought my own sheets. You'll find them on the top inside my trunk."

Lydia quickly made up the bed as Granny, groaning with each step, hobbled toward the room. Lydia waited as Granny eased herself to the narrow bed and pulled a pink afghan around her shoulders then slipped away, hurrying to peel the vegetables and work on supper preparations. She couldn't remember how long Matt had said to cook everything and wished she had thought to ask Granny before letting her escape to her room, but now it was too late and she would have to do her best.

Granny shuffled out when the men returned. They seated themselves around the table and Matt reached for the bowl of potatoes.

Sam cleared his throat.

Matt jerked back and glanced at Sam.

Sam nodded in Lydia's direction and Matt mumbled, "Forgot." Then he smiled thinly at Lydia. "Would you like to pray before we eat?"

Lydia nodded and again said a quick prayer of thanks.

Granny barely waited until Lydia said, "Amen," before she began.

"I declare. Mr. Arness always said the grace." She glowered at one man and then the other. "It just isn't fitting for a young gal to be saying the prayer when there's two perfectly capable men here. Why don't one of you give thanks?"

Sam drummed his fingertips on the tabletop and stared out the window.

Matt glowered at Granny. "Well now, I expect I could say the words as well as anybody. I just don't care to. Lydia, on the other hand, said right up front she thought it should be done, so I'll leave it to her." He grabbed the potatoes and spooned some onto his plate.

"Well, I do declare. It just doesn't seem right."

Lydia shrank back, wishing the floor would swallow her. She hadn't intended to start a fuss. She was quite sure it didn't matter to God who said what, but it didn't seem right not to say grace seeing they were dependent on God's provision.

The meat was tough, the biscuits underbaked, and the potatoes still hard in the middle, but the men ate the food without complaint. Granny only pecked at hers, her tongue stilled for the time being.

When the men were done, Sam held his coffee cup and smiled as he glanced around the room.

"I'd forgotten there was a desk under that pile of papers." He nodded. "Good-looking desk, too." He slanted a look at Lydia. "What'd you do with all the papers?"

She guessed they'd be nervous about her throwing out something important. "I sorted them into piles. Anything that looked like business, I put into the drawers." Most of the drawers held odd bits of tools and hardware and she'd put that in a box and shoved it under the bottom shelf in the pantry. "I put all the old newspapers in a bundle." First, she'd gone through the newer ones hoping to find someone needing a housekeeper or nanny or companion; but there was nothing and she had swallowed her disappointment.

Matt stretched and yawned. "What do you think?" he asked Sam. "Have I got time for a nap or shall we go finish that fence?"

Sam jumped to his feet. "The fence." And he grabbed up his hat and headed for the door.

Matt chuckled. "Wouldn't do to spend the evening lolly-gagging about," he explained to Lydia, winking as he followed Sam out the door.

Lydia pressed her palms to her hot cheeks hoping Granny had not seen. *What would Mrs. Williams have said?* Then she stiffened and carried the dishes to the basin. *Who cares what Mrs. Williams and her husband might think? They hadn't cared much for propriety when they sent me to this job.*

Granny nursed her tea and watched as Lydia cleared up and washed the dishes. Lydia finished and hung the rag over the basin.

Granny spoke without breaking the rhythm of her rocking. "You didn't rinse that rag out."

Lydia stared at it then, sighing, poured a little cold water in the basin and rinsed it well before she again draped it over the edge.

"How did you manage to get yourself into this mess?" Granny demanded as Lydia cut the leftover meat into a large pot and set it aside to stew.

Lydia stiffened. Granny made it sound like it was her fault. Remembering her vow of kindness, she took a deep breath before she answered. "I understood I was to be working for a family."

Granny snorted. "Two less family-minded men you couldn't have found."

Lydia turned to stare at her. "What do you mean?"

Fixing her pale eyes on Lydia's face, she answered, "From what I hear of them they don't have time for anything but work." She paused and added darkly, "I've heard other things, too."

Lydia's stomach lurched. They seemed pleasant enough young men. "What have you heard?"

Granny appeared to think better of what she had begun and pressed her lips tight.

Lydia persisted. "If there's some dark secret, I should know about it."

Granny shook her head. "It's no dark secret and besides, now that I think about it, it was a long time ago. Before Sam came." She halted, but when Lydia continued to stare at her, she went on. "I can't say for sure if it was right or not, but I heard stories about Matt being a bit wild. But like I say, that was a while back. Haven't heard any rumors recently so maybe it was an exaggeration or could be he learned his lesson. Many a fine man has had a wild youth." She rushed on. "In his favor, I understand he is honest and hardworking. The men all speak highly of him. And the women find him charming."

Lydia tucked away a smile at the way Granny said the final words—like it was something to dread.

"And Sam?"

Granny shrugged. "My guess is Sam isn't interested in much but work." She pursed her lips. "Maybe he's running from a broken heart or something."

This time Lydia made no attempt to hide her grin. She was beginning to suspect Granny spent a great deal of her time speculating about other people.

Granny seemed inclined to linger and watch Lydia work. With several hours left before dark, Lydia decided to keep working on the kitchen and heated a bucket of water then set to work scrubbing the rest of the floor, the rhythmic creak of Granny's rocker keeping her company.

"Sam tells me you came over from England."

It wasn't a question, but Lydia recognized the bid for more information. She worked as she talked. "That's right. I came with Reverend Williams and his wife and children, Annie, Harry, and Grace. I've worked for the family since Gracie was a baby." She missed the children so much she ached.

Grabbing the scrub brush with both hands, she shoved it back and forth, back and forth, determined to ignore the pain their memory brought.

Granny grunted. "At least you're young. No doubt you'll find someone to marry you and take care of you. Me, I'm too old for that. Besides, I could never stand to live with another man. Not after my Will." She sighed. "But it's no fun depending on others to provide you with a home."

Lydia sat back on her heels and flexed her aching arms. She wished she could offer some sort of encouragement, but Granny's words came too close to echoing her own feelings, and yet hearing the bitterness in the older woman's voice made her think. She didn't want to end up a prune-mouthed old maid. "I'm sure God will provide something for you." She dipped the brush into the hot water and mumbled under her breath, "And me."

"Yes, yes, of course." The chair rocked faster. A few minutes later Granny pushed to her feet. "It's time I put these old bones in bed." She left with a muttered good-night.

Lydia had dumped out the last of the dirty water and rinsed the rags before Sam and Matt tramped back in.

They jerked to a stop.

"I guess we should clean our boots before we come in," Sam mumbled, and they went back out, returning in a few minutes with most of the dirt scraped off.

Matt grinned as he hung his hat on a nail. "You sure are making progress getting this place cleaned up. It looks good."

"Thanks," she mumbled, a great weariness falling about her shoulders. She looked longingly at the bedroom door. Was it polite to excuse herself and go to bed? She yawned and rubbed her eyes and decided she couldn't wait another minute to think about the correct thing. "If you'll excuse me, I'm going to bed." She left without a backward look.

A few minutes later she heard the men cross to their room.

In her nightdress she sat on her bed, loneliness pressing into her chest. *If only there were a place where I belonged. A little corner of the world I could call my own.* When her mother was alive they'd had two little rooms of their own. Now she had nothing. She would go from this house to another and another, always moving when her services were no longer needed. She ached for a family where she could become a permanent part.

Granny had predicted marriage would end her dilemma, but she knew it was a futile dream. No man would ever look at her and choose her for a wife. Not with her plain brown hair, her pale gray eyes, and her equally plain face. Mother had often said she had a face that would stand the test of time. "You'll only get more and more beautiful," she'd said, but Lydia knew she saw with eyes of love.

She picked up the Bible. Mother had told her over and over

that God would take care of her. Lydia sighed. She knew she should be grateful for small mercies and in a sense she was. This place was pleasant enough, it felt safe now that Granny was here, and the men seemed to appreciate even her faltering efforts.

But despite her attempts to remain strong in her faith and trust God to provide what was best, she couldn't stop the emptiness that sucked at her strength. Shivers raced up and down her arms and she crawled into bed, pulling the quilt tightly to her chin.

She slept poorly and woke with little energy.

Granny snored softly from her bedroom during breakfast.

Matt glanced at the door. "Is she going to sleep all day?" he muttered.

"I don't think she had a good night," Lydia murmured. "I heard her up several times." Her head ached. She was grateful the men hurried out without wasting time with conversation.

She forced her weary limbs to do her bidding as she cleared up the kitchen and set to work scrubbing walls. She'd added vegetables to the leftover meat and the mixture simmered on the stove.

Granny hobbled from her room as the men returned for lunch.

Matt took a deep breath as he pulled a chair to the table. "Smells good in here." She noticed he picked up a biscuit and opened it gingerly. When he saw it was cooked clear through, he nodded. Looking up, he caught her watching him and grinned. "You're a quick learner."

With an answering smile, she said, "Thank you." Then as a warmth crept up her neck, she dipped her head.

Sam sighed as he tried a spoonful of stew. "Excellent," he mumbled. "It is great to come in to a hot meal."

They truly seemed to appreciate her efforts, and smoothness settled into the pit of her stomach.

Sam pushed to his feet. "We'll be gone most of the afternoon checking fences. Don't work too hard." He smiled at Lydia before he ducked out the door.

Matt grinned at her as he slapped his hat on his head. "Well now, Miss Lydia, Sam's right. You don't need to do everything the first day or two. There's plenty of time. You might as well enjoy life. Go outside for a walk or read a book or something."

Granny snorted as they left. "Men. What do they know about a woman's work?" She glared at the living room that Lydia had yet to tackle. "It's obvious these two think a house cleans itself." She pumped back and forth in her rocker. "Get me my knitting bag, Lydia. It's by my bed."

Lydia blinked at Granny's command. Not even so much as a "please." But she dredged up a smile and hurried to do as ordered. As she watched Granny's gnarled fingers plucking at the yarn, she forgot her resentment. Granny was right. At least Lydia was young and strong.

She hurried with the dishes then turned to face Granny. "Matt's right. The housework will keep. I'm going to go outside for a while."

Granny frowned. "Neglected work multiplies," she muttered, but Lydia only smiled.

"I'll get it done soon enough." She hurried outdoors before Granny could say anything more.

A few steps from the house she halted and turned full circle. The cloudless blue sky was almost blinding in its brightness. The sunshine warmed her veins.

She'd always lived in town, and apart from glimpses from the train window, this was the first time she'd seen such an expanse of space. She was a dot in the vast panorama of rolling green hills. She looked about and, seeing no one, lifted her hands above her head and twirled. Breathless, she paused, and, catching a glimpse of purple down the slope, slid down to investigate, sinking to the soft grass where downy, bell-like purple flowers waved in the breeze. As she marveled at their grace, a rustle startled her and she turned to see a motionless tweed-brown rabbit with flattened ears. Lydia laughed.

At the sound of her voice, it bounced away.

She looked at the lake far below, its surface rippled by a tickling breeze. Big Spring Lake—she knew from listening to the men. She threw back her head to take a deep breath of the cool air laden with spicy grass smells, and drawing her knees to her chest, hugged her arms around them.

For the first time in so long she couldn't remember, she found her world worth embracing.

She breathed deeply. If only she could feel this way every day. If she could feel this good about the future. She sat still and quiet for a long time then rose and ambled back to the house.

Granny had gone to her room when Lydia returned. Humming quietly, enjoying the solitude, Lydia set to work washing the kitchen windows. That done, she began removing items from the wall in the living room and dusting the logs.

❧

Lydia stood washing dishes the next morning, thinking about meal preparations and the work she'd do today as Sam and Matt sat at the table discussing their plans. Granny had again failed to come to breakfast.

Sam's voice startled her from her contemplation. "Why don't you take Lydia with you? I'm sure she'd enjoy it."

"Good idea!" Matt turned to her. "Would you like to come?"

Lydia looked from one to the other. "I'm sorry, I wasn't listening. Where are you going?"

"I'm headed up in the hills for some firewood. Do you want to come along and see the best part of the countryside?"

She hesitated for a moment, finding herself tongue-tied at the thought of being alone with him. But the beauty of the outdoors called. She wanted to see more of this country. "I'd like that." She kept her head down to hide the color she felt rising in her cheeks.

"Good." Matt rose to leave. "I'll be back as soon as I hitch up the wagon."

Lydia hurriedly scribbled a note telling Granny she was going exploring. A few minutes later she sat high in her perch on the wagon seat turning from side to side trying to take in everything. Matt was quick to notice her interest.

"See the crocuses over there?" He pointed to her side of the wagon. "They're like a bridge between winter and spring. Seems like they come out before winter decides to leave and stay until spring is really here.

"Look, there are some buffalo beans." He stopped the wagon and jumped down to pick a handful of lemon-colored flowers, handing them up to Lydia.

A lump swelled in her throat as she buried her face in them and peeked at him from under her eyelashes. He climbed back to his place beside her, the seat bouncing as he sat down, but he didn't spare her a glance before he flicked the team into a steady walk. Despite his impersonal interest she couldn't help feeling it was a special time as he continued to point out plants of the area—the silver willow bathing them in spicy perfume, the olive-colored sage, the wild pussy willows, and the poplars dressed in palest green buds.

Granny was right. Matt could be quite charming when he chose.

The trail grew more uneven, and he fell silent, concentrating on guiding the horses over the rough ground.

"Where does this trail go?" Lydia asked as it grew more rugged.

"It's the trail we made last summer to get logs out of the hills to build on to the house."

The living room with its logs was quite different in construction from the frame kitchen, Granny's little room, and the long bedroom the men shared. "You built the log part of the house after the rest?"

"Well, the house was pretty small when we bought the place

from Old Man Burrdges. We wanted more room for ourselves and a room for a housekeeper, so we split the house in half and added the front room and your room in the middle."

"How long have you and Sam been living here?"

"I was here before Sam, running horses in the hills and helping Old Man Burrdges. We bought the place over a year ago now."

"Where did you come from before that?" Suddenly there were so many things she wanted to know about him.

"From a lot of different places." Matt said it like it was all the explanation necessary, but Lydia persisted.

"Like where, for instance?"

"Well, I worked for a rancher in North Dakota for a while. Before that I did some tinsmithing. I even helped build bridges for a while."

Lydia turned on the hard seat to look at him more carefully. He kept his eyes on the horses, giving them more attention than she thought they needed.

"Where did you come from to start with?"

Matt's face hardened. "I was born in Wisconsin."

"Is that where your family is?"

"I have no family ties." He shook the reins as if to indicate that the conversation was over.

She folded her hands in her lap and stared straight ahead. Many times she had experienced the same reluctance to discuss her family with strangers. Her hands clenched in her lap. Perhaps he was hiding a shameful secret.

For a few minutes they rode in silence, then Matt leaned back and looked at Lydia. "What about you; where are you from?"

She didn't mind telling him and relaxed. "I was born in Witnesham, Suffolk, England."

"I understand that you have no family. I'm sorry. What happened?"

The kindness in his voice brought tightness to Lydia's throat. She swallowed hard then told how she had lost both parents, then about living with the Williams family and coming to Canada with them. She explained how she'd had to move on when Annabelle decided to emigrate.

"That must have been hard after so long with them and no family here." Matt shook his head. "No wonder you were angry at ending up with us."

"Well," Lydia tilted her head and considered him, "one good thing came out of it."

"What would that be? Perhaps that you have two fine fellows to look after you?"

"Nooo. That's not what I had in mind." She shook her head and looked around at the beauty enfolding them. "I got to come to Canada. It is such a wild, free land." She sighed. "I'm just glad I could come."

"Then I think you'll enjoy what I have to show you."

The wagon climbed a steep grade with trees pressing in on either side.

"It's just over that rise." He pointed toward the break in the trees.

"What is it?" Excitement touched Lydia's voice.

"You'll see in a minute. It's worth waiting for, you can be sure."

They broke through the trees and drove a few yards more before Matt pulled the wagon to a halt. Quickly, he jumped down and ran to help Lydia. Grabbing her hand, he pulled her toward the edge of the hill then stopped. "Look." He waved his arm.

Before Lydia lay a scene so enormous that she gasped and stared openmouthed.

The tree-covered hills fell away before her in gentle waves to the deep blue of Big Spring Lake, surrounded by its collar of white. Beyond lay the plains, rippling on and on until they disappeared into a smoky gray line at the horizon.

Lydia's eyes felt wide. "I think I've just seen infinity," she whispered.

"Come, that's not all." He turned her around and pulled her past the wagon to the other side of the plateau. Again she saw the vast landscape open before her. This side of the hills lacked the beauty of the lake, and the plains were dotted with dark patches of bushes, but again, Lydia felt she could see forever.

After a few minutes she swallowed and glanced toward Matt.

He was staring at the scene before them. Sensing her eyes on him, he turned. "You are standing on the Neutral Hills. They are called that because the Cree Indians lived to the north." He pointed to the plains before them. "And the Blackfoot to the south." He pointed to the far edge. "From these hills the tribes could come and spot game—deer, buffalo, whatever—then go out and hunt it. For that reason, they agreed this would be a place either tribe could come without fear of attack from the other.

"Come on. There's more." He pulled her after him down the trail. The plateau widened, the trees still sheltering the edge. Matt stopped. "See those circles of rocks?"

Lydia nodded.

"Those are tepee rings. They're the rocks the Indians used to hold down the edges of their tepees."

Lydia looked about her. There were several rings where she stood. "Do the Indians come here anymore?"

"No. Not since the buffalo disappeared and they signed treaties agreeing to live on reservations." He stood pensive for several seconds. "It's too bad to see a way of life end like that."

As she followed Matt back to the wagon, Lydia thought of the mysterious inhabitants who had lived in such a different way. It seemed strange to see signs of them, yet not one living being.

They continued along the hill to a small draw where Matt pulled the wagon to a halt. In the trees was a pile of logs, all trimmed and neatly stacked. Matt jumped down and crossed to

Lydia's side. "I'll be busy awhile if you want to go exploring."

Looking down on his broad smile and twitching mustache, Lydia felt a warmth building in the region of her heart. Whatever secret his past held, he was an interesting man with a kind, generous way about him.

And right now he'd be wondering what took her so long to respond. She allowed him to grasp her around the waist and lift her from the wagon. She stood facing him, his hands still at her waist, and breathed deeply, her senses assailed by the masculine scent of him. And then he released her and strode to the pile of wood and heaved an armload into the wagon.

Her gaze followed him, lingering on the muscles that bulged in his arms and down his back. Then she shepherded her thoughts and set off to explore.

She found many spots where she could view the plains below. She thrilled to the majesty before her. She was looking down a narrow valley with a stream glistening like a silver ribbon when she heard the wagon approach.

"It's a great view, isn't it?" Matt called out as he waited for her to join him. "I never get tired of it. Sometimes I come up here just to have a look. Never fails to make me feel better somehow."

"It's wonderful. I'll never forget it." Lydia faced Matt. "I want to thank you for bringing me." Without waiting for a reply, she turned quickly and let him help her up, smoothing her skirts neatly around her as she sat.

Before he flicked the reins, Matt nodded toward her. "I'm glad you enjoyed it."

The ride down the hill was more difficult because of the decline and the load in the wagon. For a time neither of them spoke, but crossing the same ground took Lydia's thoughts back to the conversation they had on the upward trip.

"How did you and Sam meet?"

"Sam was looking for someplace to start a farm or ranch and met Old Man Burrdges in town. They got to talking and

Burrdges invited him to come to his ranch. That was when Sam and I met. Turns out Old Man Burrdges thought this country was getting too civilized. Said he wanted to go west and live out in the mountains, so we decided to buy him out."

"Where did Sam come from?"

"Little Miss Curiosity!" He smiled as he said it. "I know he came from England and has family back there. 'Fraid I don't know too much more about him. We sort of agreed to mind our own business with each other. Guess if you want to know, you'll have to ask him yourself."

Lydia lapsed into a thoughtful silence. She would, indeed, find a time to talk to Sam about his family and background, and hopefully he would reveal more than Matt had.

Matt circled past the house and let Lydia off before he drove to the shed to unload the wood.

The house was quiet when she entered; Granny, no doubt, was sleeping in her room.

Humming, she put on the coffee pot and went to the pantry to get vegetables. As she moved about she decided she liked Matt. She was pleased that he'd been willing to share his favorite place with her.

She heard the wagon rumble across the yard then the barn door squeal as it was opened. The coffee boiled and she pushed it to the back of the stove. A few minutes later Matt entered and bent over the basin to wash. He was drying on the towel when Sam burst through the door.

"Matt, come quick! Queenie's had her foal and she's brought him to the fence to show him off." He hurried back outside then stopped and called. "He's a beauty. Hurry before she leaves."

Matt grabbed his hat. Sam shifted from foot to foot, his gaze roaming restlessly around the room and, seeing Lydia standing at the stove, said, "You, too, Lydia. Come and see the foal."

Lydia didn't need a second invitation and hurried after them.

At the pasture fence stood a black horse, neighing as they approached. Lydia and Matt held back as Sam went to her, murmuring compliments. He climbed the fence slowly and stepped down on the other side. The foal skittered away on long, awkward legs then stopped and watched as Sam stroked Queenie and talked to her, all the while keeping his eyes on the nervous foal. For a few minutes he watched, his eyes reflecting his pleasure. Then he quietly backed away.

"Isn't he a beauty?" he asked, his voice warm and rich.

"Looks like he's got the makings of a good horse," Matt agreed. "You did okay with that mare."

"She's got good bloodlines." He turned to Lydia. "Isn't he something?"

"He sure is." But she watched Sam, not the foal. His blue eyes sparkled, his face shone with pleasure, and he bounced on the balls of his feet. She had never seen him so animated. It filled him with a vitality that made her throat constrict.

After a few minutes they returned to the house. Lydia poured coffee for the men and drank hers as she continued supper preparations.

Sam talked more than she'd ever heard him, racing on about the shed they would build, the fences that needed to be extended, and the herd of horses that would result from Queenie and her foal. There was a timbre to his voice that plucked at Lydia's heartstrings. She stole a glance at him. He scrubbed his fingers through his hair as he talked, the movement highlighting strands streaked with sunlight. His eyes flashed. She hadn't noticed before what a vivid shade of blue they were. She blinked. He was quite handsome when he was excited about something.

three

The next morning, breakfast cleaned up, Lydia carried a bucket of hot water to the living room and tackled the smoke-grimed windows. She completed the first one and leaned against the sill letting the morning sunshine warm her. The outdoors danced with light, making her feet restless. Sighing, she turned away and, squeezing her rag out, began scrubbing the next pane. Each swipe made the outdoors appear brighter and closer and let in more of the enticing sunshine.

"Come here," Granny called from her room.

Lydia dropped the rag and stepped to the door. "Good morning. What can I do for you?"

Granny groaned. "There's a hot water bottle at the bottom of the bed. Fill it up again." She tipped her head back. "My old bones are making a real fuss today. I doubt I'll be able to get out of bed. You'll have to bring me my tea."

Lydia blinked. Annoyance threatened to erupt into anger until she saw the sun glaring under the lowered blind. She smiled, promising herself to let nothing ruin her enjoyment of the day. "I'm sorry you're feeling poorly," she murmured as she retrieved the hot water bottle.

Granny groaned. "Sometimes I think I must have done something really bad to have to suffer so. God is punishing me."

Lydia gaped at the older lady. If Granny had decided suffering meant God no longer loved her, it was no wonder she was often cranky. She thought of her mother who had suffered so much the last year of her life but still had remained sweet and gentle. Feeling half-guilty, half-pleased, Lydia knew it was because Mother was so intent on preparing Lydia for the future that she didn't have time to linger on her pain. *No, it*

was more than that. Mother never wavered in her belief that
God had a bigger picture in mind. "Troubles can either make
us bitter, or better," she'd said.

Lydia looked down on Granny, wanting so much to communicate the assurance of God's loving control that she'd learned from Mother. "My mother used to tell me that our lives are like a weaving. We see only the bottom side, but God uses the dark strands, as well as the light, to create a beautiful picture."

Granny grunted. "Just get me what I asked for."

As Lydia filled the bottle and made a pot of tea, her own words circled round and round in her head. For a while she'd forgotten to trust God's love, but she promised herself she would not let her light and momentary troubles push her away from God but, rather, draw her closer to Him.

She left Granny settled with the hot water bottle at her back and a tea tray on a low table next to her bed and returned to her task to find the water had grown cold. As she dumped it out, Matt came to the door and called, "We're heading out to the pasture. Could you throw a few things together for a lunch?" He hesitated at the door, his wide smile lifting the corners of his mustache. "I don't suppose you know how to make bread?" Then he shook his head. "No, I suppose not, and I'm guessing Granny won't ever feel up to giving you a lesson either." His dark gaze lingered on Granny's closed door. "Fresh bread would sure be welcome around here." He shrugged and nodded toward the pantry. "Throw in a handful of those dried apples from the corner cupboard." The door banged and he was gone.

Lydia slapped together biscuits and jam. She wrapped a handful of dried apples and threw everything into a sack. When Matt came to the door she handed him the bag.

As soon as they rode out of sight she set aside the bucket. Windows were easily forgotten when the outdoors called, and being careful not to disturb Granny, she slipped into the sunshine.

She hurried toward the hill where she slid down the bank to a ledge and sat in the fragrant grass staring at the lake shimmering in the bright sun. A gentle breeze lifted her hair and filled her senses with a mixture of alluring scents: sage grass and the nectar of flowers, the dry heat of the distant prairie and the warmth of the sky.

The first words of the Bible sang through her mind, "In the beginning God created the heaven and the earth." The words echoed like a drum beat. "In the beginning. . . In the beginning. . . ." They pulsated through her until the assurance that God was there from the beginning and would certainly be here for her now beat into her heart.

The words grew louder and louder until she realized it was the sound of wheels she heard. A wagon drove into the yard. Her gaze darted about searching for a place to hide, and with a mouth gone as dry as cotton, she settled for huddling down in the grass, hoping she was invisible from the house.

The rattle of the wheels, the snort of a horse, and a sharp "whoa" came to her. A pause and then Lydia heard the rap of knuckles on the door. She huddled down as far as she could, hardly daring to breathe.

"Hello, is anyone home?" It was a woman's voice and Lydia released a ragged breath, jumping to her feet to climb the hill.

Her visitor's voice rose as she called again, "Hello? Where are you? I'm your next door neighbor come to visit." She turned and saw Lydia. "There you are!" In the yard stood a sturdy young woman.

Lydia walked across to her. "I'm sorry I wasn't here when you knocked." She reached around the girl and opened the door. "Won't you please come in and have tea? I'm Lydia Baxter."

The girl removed her bonnet and shook free her blond hair. "I'm pleased to meet you. I'm Alice Young and I guess I'd be about your nearest neighbor. The boys stopped by this afternoon and told me about you coming here."

"The boys?"

Alice nodded. "Matt and Sam. They came by on their way up to the pasture. Said they thought you could use some company." She hurried on before Lydia could answer. "I know I sure can." She glanced around the room. "I thought they said Granny Arness was here."

Lydia jerked her head in the direction of Granny's room. "She's feeling poorly today and said she was staying in bed."

Lydia tried to sort the information Alice had imparted. "Where do you live?"

"Down the road a bit. You pass our place on the way to Akasu."

"I don't remember noticing it."

"No, you wouldn't." Alice smiled. "You can only see it from the other direction." Then she rushed on. "Norman and I have been married three months. I'm happy to be married but I still miss my folks and the younger ones. It's the first time I've been away from home." Her face grew wistful. "I wish it weren't so far. It would be nice to visit them." She sighed and shook her head. "I'm sorry. I shouldn't be troubling you with my homesickness. Tell me about yourself. How old are you? Where you from? Where's your family?"

Lydia began. "I'm nineteen—"

"Same as me."

Lydia nodded. "I have no family. My father died when I was a baby. I don't even remember him. My mother died six years ago. Since then I've been a servant for a number of families. I came to Canada two years ago with the Williams family."

She told Alice about having to leave when a niece wanted to come to Canada.

Alice, in turn, told about being the eldest of six children and how she had met Norman while he worked for a neighbor. She told how Norman came to Alberta, picked out a quarter of land, and built a sod shanty before going back to marry Alice.

For a moment neither spoke, lost in memories of the separate roads that led them to their present situation.

Lydia gasped. "I'm sorry, I haven't made us any tea yet." She jumped to her feet and scurried around.

Alice opened the bag on her lap. "Sam said he thought you could use some help with recipes so I brought along my cookbook." She held a worn book with loose pages bulging out. "It used to be my mother's." She dashed away a tear then dipped into her bag and drew out a small paper-wrapped package. "I hope you don't mind," she murmured glancing at Lydia. "I thought I would give you a lesson in making bread."

Lydia laughed. "Matt's suggestion, I suspect."

Alice giggled. "It was indeed."

Tea was again forgotten as Alice showed her how to make bread. It was a lot more fun than Lydia expected as Alice took her through every step. Lydia laughed as she watched the yeast foam up as if it had a mind of its own. Alice said helping Lydia reminded her of some of her own disasters, and as she shared her experiences she had them both giggling.

It was only after the dough was set aside to rise that they finally had their long-awaited tea.

"We have church in Akasu every Sunday now," Alice began. "We'd be glad to take you with us if you could get one of the boys to bring you over."

"Why that would be lovely, but—"

"I'm sure they'd bring you if you ask."

"Perhaps."

Granny shuffled from her room at that point demanding more tea and a bite to eat. She glanced at the dough rising. "I see you've done something useful with your time."

Alice looked startled as she met Lydia's gaze. Lydia shrugged. She was quickly learning to ignore Granny's sharp comments.

Her newfound friend left soon after leaving instructions on baking the loaves.

Shivering, Lydia lit the lamp and placed it on the table. The golden, fragrant loaves lay on a cloth at the other end. Darkness had closed in around the house. Granny had grunted, "Those two scallywags are up to no good. Mark my words," before she shuffled off to bed two hours ago.

Matt and Sam had still not returned.

Lydia's fears circled round and round at a fevered pitch. What had happened to them? Maybe they met an outlaw up in the hills. Or been attacked by a bear or a wolf. What if they didn't come back? What would happen to her?

Suddenly she gave a short, bitter laugh. She, who had feared the presence of the men, now feared they might not return. She admitted the second possibility held far more dangers than the first.

Unable to sit idly staring into the lamp, she jumped up and went to the stove to lift the lids on the pots. Quiet pride flowed as she stirred the mashed potatoes, now growing dark and sticky. Meat stewed in thick, rich gravy.

She dropped the lid back on the pot and turned away. She'd made such a nice meal and it was going to go to waste if they didn't get home soon. She paced to the window to stare into the blackness outside, straining to pick up some sign of movement. After a moment she returned to the table to sit huddled in front of the lamp.

Was that the sound of horses in the yard? She stood frozen while the door opened and two figures entered. Her fright changed to shock at the sight of the men.

Pale mud clung to their chaps and boots, the color reflected in their fatigue-lined faces. Matt threw his wet cowboy hat at a hook where it rested for a minute then plopped to the floor. Sam grabbed two chairs, offering one to Matt.

"Is there any hot water?" Matt asked in a voice thick with weariness.

Lydia hurried to pour water into the basin while the men

unbuckled their chaps and dropped them to the floor. Matt tugged at his boots.

"Here, I'll help." Sam got up and straddled Matt's leg. He pulled and grunted, assisted by Matt's other leg pushing at his backside until the boot came off trailing muddy water in its wake. Another struggle and Matt's other boot hit the floor. The men reversed positions and Matt pulled off Sam's wet, muddy boots.

"Lydia, run to our room and get us some dry clothes, would you?" asked Matt as he pulled off his wet socks and began to unbutton his shirt.

Her face burning, Lydia lit another lamp and went to fetch the needed items. Both men were stripped to their jeans when she returned. For a moment they looked blankly at her, then Sam said slowly, "Maybe you should wait in your room until we get changed and washed."

She fled, waiting in the darkness until Sam called, "It's all right now. You can come out."

He lay sprawled in the big armchair in the front room. Matt stood before the corner cupboard pouring amber liquid into two small glasses. He offered one to Sam and kept the other as he sank into the soft couch. He took a slow drink from his glass, meeting Lydia's eyes as he lowered his hand. She knew by the twitch of his mustache that he'd heard her sniff of disapproval and could read the severe expression on her face. She bit her tongue to keep from pointing out the evils of drink.

"I have supper made if you care for some," she said, her voice tight.

Sam sighed wearily. "I'm too tired to eat. Give us a few minutes to rest." He sank farther into the chair. "A cup of tea would sure taste good about now, though."

Matt put his glass on the floor beside his feet and slouched down, his legs stretched out in a long lazy line. "I think coffee would better fit the bill, but make the Englishman his tea and I'll share it with him."

They remained motionless, heads back and eyes shut, as Lydia hurried to boil the water.

"I have never seen such a stupid cow in all my life," Matt said, his voice low and lazy.

"The way she acted you'd think we were trying to butcher her not rescue her." Sam moaned as he shifted, turning to Lydia with an explanation. "A rangy old cow got stuck in a mud hole. Looked like she'd been there since yesterday. But she put up such a fight when we tried to get her out I thought we'd all three end up drowned in the mud before we could free her."

"She sure took off in a high fury when she got free," Matt laughed. "I expect she'll stay clear of us for a long time."

"Suits me just fine." Sam stretched and moaned again. "Think I'll have some supper then go to bed. I'm completely exhausted."

Lydia hurried to the stove to serve up plates of food. The men ate quickly and silently then shuffled to their room.

Deciding it had been a long day for her as well, she put the dishes in the basin and poured water over them, leaving them to soak until morning, then dragged herself to her room and crawled into bed where she lay staring into the dark. Matt's drinking disturbed her and she couldn't understand why. She'd been in homes before where it had been a part of celebrations and she had simply turned away and ignored it, so why should this time be different? Why should it make her want to cry?

Next morning, the men moved slowly, rubbing sore spots on their legs and stretching their back muscles.

"Did you have to use up all the hot water?" Matt shook the kettle and stared down its spout.

"Sorry. Put some more on. It'll only take a few minutes."

Matt grumbled to himself as he filled the kettle and put it on the hottest spot on the stove.

"My boots are still wet," Sam grumbled. "Now I'll have to wear my good ones."

"Ain't my fault," Matt retorted.

"Never said it was."

"Breakfast is ready," Lydia murmured, hoping they wouldn't turn their grumbling to her.

They hunched over their places, eating in grumpy silence. Lydia watched them warily, almost expecting them to growl over their food.

"If we had a dog he could've chased that old cow out all by himself." Sam kept his head bent over his bowl.

Matt slammed his fist into the table. "I won't have a dog on the place. They can be more trouble than help." He shoved his chair back and gathered his coat. "You know how I feel."

"Yeah. I know." Sam sighed, making no effort to hide his exasperation.

Lydia had been about to mention how pleasantly the sun was shining, and didn't it look like a nice day? But she bit back her comment, remembering how often she'd let herself think there was nothing to be happy about.

She stood gazing out the window with her hands in warm dishwater and examined her thoughts. How often had she turned her face from what was good to hunker over the bad, tending it like a reluctant fire?

Too often, she admitted. It was a lovely day with the sun on the spring-green hills, and the view from the window was pleasant. She breathed a prayer of thanks.

The following days could have been cut from the same cloth.

Each evening the men returned late—tired and dirty, though never as late and dirty as the first evening. In the morning, they were short-tempered and testy with each other. Lydia was thankful they chose to ignore her except to call for hot water or give instructions for the evening meal.

Granny spent most of each day in her room, nursing a hot water bottle, or shuffled out to sit in her rocker picking at her knitting and offering dire comments about life.

Lydia found the days long and boring.

The sun was almost directly overhead several days later when Lydia heard the rattle and creak of a horse and wagon entering the yard. A quick glance out the window showed Alice stopping in front of the house. Before she could step down from her perch, Lydia threw open the door and bounded out. "Am I ever glad to see you! I was getting very bored with my own company."

Alice laughed. "Sounds like the lament of many a prairie woman. Have the boys been away?"

"Well, not exactly." Lydia pulled her toward the house. "They've been moving cattle up to the pasture in the hills and have been gone all day. And when they are home they're as cross as a couple of dogs with noses full of porcupine quills."

Alice laughed at the wry face Lydia pulled. "I wondered what happened to you yesterday. I fully expected to see you for church."

Lydia felt her mouth drop. "I plumb forgot what day it was. Fact is, I've hardly spoken to either of them, nor they to me. It doesn't seem to be worth it. Neither of them has said a polite word in days."

"That's a bit odd. They're always pleasant to be around and seem such good friends. Perhaps they're having some problems."

Lydia nodded. "They've said something about having trouble getting some cows out of a coulee. I think the side of a hill slid down in the spring rains and trapped them. They sounded like they might finish up today or tomorrow, though."

From what Lydia could gather from overheard comments, that would complete the task of moving the cows to spring pasture. Her heart swelled knowing they would soon have to make good on their promise to take her back to town. Perhaps Alice could suggest a better position for her.

"How did your bread turn out?"

"It was fine. I've made it three times now and it's turned out good each time." She shook her head. "Not that anyone seems to notice. Neither of them said a word, though they manage to eat large quantities of it."

"Then it's being appreciated, isn't it?" Alice smiled.

"I suppose you're right. Now tell me about church."

Alice entertained Lydia with comments about the people at church and the happenings of the small town of Akasu.

"I'm curious," said Lydia. "Akasu is such an unusual name. Where did it come from?"

"Norman tells me it's a Cree word meaning sick. He says it's because the water from Big Spring Lake is full of alkali and makes animals and people sick if they drink it."

Lydia nodded. "Matt told me a bit about the Cree and Blackfoot."

"Far as I know there aren't many around anymore. Now tell me what you've been doing."

Soon Lydia was telling how she had spent the long, lonely afternoons exploring the countryside just outside her door. The wide open spaces stirred something deep within her soul. She couldn't describe the feeling, not even to herself. She felt her heart expanding as if to embrace the vastness of the landscape.

The view from the hills continually beckoned. From her perch, she could look down on the lake and watch both cattle and wild animals grazing nearby. She thrilled to the delightful surprises she found hidden in the grass. "The crocuses are beautiful."

"I know. They turn whole pastures into a purple carpet in the spring. And it doesn't have to be very warm either."

"Matt says they're the bridge between winter and spring."

Alice laughed. "I didn't realize he was so poetic." She shrugged. "I guess I shouldn't be surprised. He does seem to have a way with words, though in the time I've known him I still don't really know a lot about him." Her expression grew thoughtful. "It's like he has this surface that is all charm and good cheer, yet sometimes I get the feeling that's all it is—surface—and underneath it all is a very serious, deep-thinking man." With a little chuckle she shook her head. "And here I am writing my own story as my mother often said."

Lydia blinked. She got much the same feeling with Matt. "Sam is quieter but doesn't give away anything more than Matt."

Alice nodded. "The strong, silent type—both of them, but someday each of them will find someone they know they can trust their hearts to and that's when they'll be willing to open up." Her gaze settled thoughtfully on Lydia for a moment; then her expression grew soft. "That's the way it is with Norman. He tells me everything."

Long after Alice had left for home, the conversation stuck in Lydia's mind. Alice's words had stirred up restless longings. When Mother was alive, Lydia had known the kind of relationship Alice meant. Lydia stared out the window rubbing her palm back and forth over the ledge. Her chest muscles tightened so she could barely breathe. She exhaled loudly and jerked away, rushing to find some pressing task.

❧

Early the next afternoon the men rode into the yard, laughing companionably together, all impatience forgotten. Alice was right. They had been concerned about the cows; their friendship had survived the strain of the last few days.

They leisurely unsaddled their horses and spent a good half hour rubbing them down before they treated them to a bucket of oats. Lydia smiled. It looked like they were apologizing to their horses for their recent bad behavior.

In the house, they filled a boiler with water and put it on the stove. When it was hot, they carried it to their bedroom.

"Who goes first?" asked Sam.

"You go ahead while I clean my boots and chaps." Matt was already gathering up leather soap and rags for the job.

After Sam came from the bedroom, his hair wet and slicked back and his skin noticeably pink, they emptied the tub and refilled it for Matt.

A little later Matt emerged, his dark hair likewise wet and slicked back, his mustache trimmed and neat. Within a few minutes his hair lost its prim look as it dried into a wavy mass.

Their good humor with each other seemed completely restored.

"I feel like a new man," boasted Matt.

"Sure hope you smell like one, too," Sam teased, punching him playfully on the shoulder. "It was getting pretty painful riding downwind from you."

Matt grabbed his shoulder in mock pain. "Why do you think I was always upwind? It weren't roses I smelled coming from your direction."

They took the coffee Lydia offered and sat at the kitchen table.

Granny, hearing the noise, had come from her room and sat rocking. Lydia put a cup of coffee close to her. Her mouth pursed, Granny studied the two men. "Am I to assume you finally have the cows moved wherever it was you had to move them?"

"Yes, ma'am." Sam sighed. "And mighty glad I am to have the job done."

"And all the cows safe and sound," Matt added.

"Humph. Seems like a lot of fuss and bother for some old cows."

Sam leaned back and grinned at her. "With cows you get out of them what you put into them."

Her lips tight and working in and out, Granny turned back to her knitting.

For several minutes no one spoke as the men enjoyed their coffee and Lydia continued with supper preparations.

"Lydia?"

She jumped when Matt called her name.

"I sure hope you've got more of that homemade bread. You know, I think it's what kept us going the last few days."

Lydia felt a blush sweep up her cheeks as he continued in a teasing voice. "Just knowing our lunch would contain thick slices of it and waiting until supper for some more was worth all the hard work of the last few days. I expect we would have wasted away without it." His tone grew more serious. "Much obliged."

Sam joined in. "Yeah. Thanks for everything. You've been patient with us when there were times we were pretty awful."

Lydia mumbled, "You're welcome," and began to turn away then paused. With a spark of boldness, she said, "There were times I felt a good spanking for you both would have been in order."

The men gaped at her. They turned to each other and blinked then both let out a shout of laughter. They laughed until they had to wipe their eyes. Then, slapping their legs, they laughed some more.

Lydia kept her back toward them, her shoulders shaking silently as she chuckled.

Over supper Matt announced, "We'll be going to town tomorrow. We can take you with us." He turned toward Granny. "You, too, of course."

Granny snorted. "And why would I be wanting to bounce myself all the way to town? I'll just make out a list and one of you can get what I need."

four

Matt turned back to Sam and they continued discussing nails and lumber for a shed while Lydia's thoughts buzzed.

She'd had the barest glimpse of the town when she arrived on the train, but it appeared a thriving center. *Surely, I will find someone who needs my services. I could work in a store, help look after children—*

"Could you make a list of supplies for the house?" Sam asked.

Startled out of her thoughts, Lydia eyed him with surprise. He regarded her with a wariness that reminded her they would be left to fend for themselves after tomorrow. The idea made her insides feel tight and she glanced around the room, now tidy and clean. How many days would it be until it was back to its former state?

She sat straighter. It didn't matter. "I know what's needed. I can make a list before we go."

"Good." His gaze rested on her for several seconds. Lydia wondered if she imagined he was waiting for her to offer to stay, but he turned to Matt without saying anything. "We better get some more paint, too."

Sleep was slow in coming that night as Lydia wondered about taking her trunk then decided to take only her valise and make arrangements for the trunk later.

God, You are finally providing a way out and I thank You. I hate to ask for more, but a job with a loving family would be nice.

She finally fell asleep with a smile on her lips, dreaming of life with a happy, generous family. She awoke with a bubble of anticipation tickling her throat and paused while making her bed to listen to the sound of birds outside the window.

Leaving her room, she saw Matt at the table, his chair tipped back as he drank a cup of coffee. She glanced back at the bedroom the men shared.

"Sam's gone to hitch up the wagon," Matt drawled, apparently enjoying his leisure while Sam did the work.

By the time Sam returned, she had made a hasty breakfast. After they'd eaten, she hurriedly washed up the dishes knowing they would otherwise sit for days and grow so hard it would be a chore to wash them. For a moment she wondered what would become of Granny. She shrugged. That wasn't her concern.

As soon as she finished, they were on their way.

"It's another nice day, isn't it?" Lydia asked as they rumbled toward town. The sun shone in a cloudless blue sky. A soft breeze teased the waving grasses, lifting the faint scent of spices. Patches of blue, yellow, and purple dotted the rippling golden-fringed grass.

The men grunted agreement.

A few minutes later Matt raised his hand and pointed to their left. "That's where Alice and Norman live."

At first Lydia couldn't see anything, then she remembered Alice said they lived in a sod shanty and realized that the brown humps were actually the house and barn. Her eyes widened and a shudder hurried up her spine.

I would hate to live in such a small, ugly house. She immediately scolded herself. Alice seemed content enough, even happy, so it couldn't be too bad. But Lydia turned away and looked straight ahead down the road. In the distance she could see a turn in the trail and strained forward trying to see everything at once.

By the time they turned the final bend before Akasu, Lydia was perched on the edge of the seat. As they drew near the town, she saw it bustled with activity.

Matt stopped in front of a building with a large wooden

sign saying Beaver Mercantile Store and helped her to the sidewalk. Across the street two ladies were deep in conversation as they entered the post office. A man laden with parcels came out of the pharmacy and crossed the street. Children ran along the sidewalk making drumming sounds with their feet. She pulled her attention back to Matt as he spoke.

"Here's twenty dollars for your wages." He handed her the bill then pointed across the street. "Sterlings Department Store carries a nice selection of ready-made ladies' wear. Why don't you go there and buy yourself a new dress—something pretty?" He climbed back onto the wagon seat and guided the horses toward the lumberyard farther down the street.

Lydia looked down at her plain, practical brown dress. She stared at her brown shoes. Suddenly she wished for a shiny black pair with fancy bows.

Sam reached out to take her elbow and Lydia jumped.

"Would you mind getting the supplies?" He guided her into the store.

"No, of course not." She'd never had the freedom to select items and relished the idea.

"You'll be able to get everything you need here."

As he went to make arrangements with the store owner, Lydia thought he must be right. Her eyes swept the shelves lining the store. They were laden with everything imaginable.

An hour later she emerged into the bright sunlight.

"I'll have it all ready to be loaded when Sam comes back," the storekeeper promised. "Thank you for your order. It's been a pleasure doing business with you."

Lydia thanked the man and allowed the door to close behind her. It had been a pleasure for her, too. She smiled and fingered the twenty dollars in her pocket. For a moment she stood and stared across the street at the sign above Sterlings Department Store.

She hesitated. What if she needed her wages to live on? But she couldn't remember ever having a new dress. She was accustomed to hand-me-downs. Her eyes narrowed and she straightened her shoulders before stepping into the street and crossing to the department store.

Inside, the ladies' wear was displayed discreetly toward the back. Lydia hurried the length of the store and lingered over the selection of dresses, hats, coats, and shoes.

"May I help you?" asked a salesgirl.

Lydia wavered for a minute then replied, "Yes, I'd like to purchase a new dress and a pair of shoes."

The girl picked out a number of dresses for Lydia's inspection.

"Let's go in the back where you can try them on," she invited. Lydia found herself in the back room being encouraged by the vivacious salesgirl, who introduced herself as Lizzie. Lydia's cheeks grew hot with the exertion of changing outfits. She studied herself in the full-length mirror. The bright dresses emphasized her gray eyes and accented her ivory complexion. Strands of dark hair had come loose from the tight roll she kept it in and softened her face. She hardly recognized herself.

"I think I like the blue one best," she said much later, indicating a soft lawn dress in light blue with darker blue flowers tumbling down the skirt. A crisp lace collar circled the neckline while dainty tucks embellished the bodice.

"You wait here and I'll find you the nicest pair of shoes you could ever want." Lizzie hurried to the front of the store. She returned as quickly as she left bearing a pair of black patent leather shoes with an attractive square heel and—Lydia drew in a sharp gasp—the daintiest black lace bow.

"Aren't these just perfect?" Lizzie asked as she slipped them onto Lydia's feet.

"Oh, yes. I'll take them."

"Why don't you wear your new dress and I'll wrap up your things?"

Lydia wavered. Before she could decide, Lizzie made up

her mind for her. "Here, I'll help you." She tucked the old dress inside a brown wrapping.

"You sit here and I'll have your hair fixed in no time," Lizzie told her.

"Oh, that isn't necessary," Lydia protested, but Lizzie gently pushed her into the chair and removed the hairpins as if Lydia hadn't spoken. Submitting, Lydia relaxed as Lizzie brushed her hair out and worked it back into place. In the mirror, she watched Lizzie pull her hair into a loose roll circling her face and secure it with a few hairpins. It gave her a soft, classy look.

"How do you like that?" asked Lizzie.

Lydia turned her head side to side, admiring the results. "I like it. Lizzie, how can I thank you? You've been such a help."

"It was fun. I like helping people find what suits them. Now away you go and have a good day."

"Wait." Lydia grasped Lizzie's arm. This was her chance. Lizzie would know where she could get a position. "Lizzie, I need a job. Do you know someone who could use my services?"

A surprised look crossed Lizzie's face. "But you have a good job."

Lydia nodded. She had told Lizzie much of her story as she tried on clothes and had her hair fixed. "I never intended to stay."

Lizzie rubbed her chin and stared at the ceiling. Lydia held her breath. There had to be something somewhere. Then Lizzie shook her head. "There's not much call for a young woman to help. Most women get married and have their job cut out for them." Her eyes narrowed as she studied Lydia carefully. "Seems to me that would answer your problem." She tipped her head and grinned. "And with that new look I'm guessing you shouldn't have any trouble."

Her jaw slack, Lydia stared at Lizzie. She wasn't ready for marriage. Why, that would mean she would have to look after a house, plan meals—she swallowed loudly. All the same things she'd been doing. But marriage? She turned and studied her reflection in the mirror. Was it really possible someone could look at her and think she'd make a good wife? As she turned from side to side she admitted she wasn't that hard to look at. Plain and practical, but weren't those desirable qualities in a wife?

Lizzie peered over her shoulder. "And you have the two most eligible bachelors in the country to choose from."

Lydia met Lizzie's eyes in the mirror. "Sam and Matt?"

Lizzie giggled. "Have you looked at them? They're so delicious-looking."

Lydia pressed her finger to her chin. Sam with his fair hair and lightning-blue eyes, Matt with that riot of dark curls and laughing mouth, yes, perhaps they were worth a second look. She grinned at Lizzie. "I guess they aren't too bad." But there was a major flaw in the whole idea; neither of them had expressed an interest in spiritual things. Mother had drummed into her that marriage was one of the biggest decisions she would ever make.

"As a Christian," she'd said, "you will never know happiness if you marry an unbeliever."

Lizzie pulled Lydia about to face her. "Where have you been, girl? Forget trying to find a job. It's next to impossible. Go take advantage of what's right before your nose."

Lydia shook her head. "No. They aren't for me."

"Why ever not? What more could you ask for?"

Lydia jerked to her feet. "When—and if—I ever marry there will be two requirements. I will have to love the man, and he must love me. And he will have to be a church-going believer." She sighed as she picked up her bundles. "Unfortunately, Sam and Matt are not." She headed toward the counter to pay for her purchases. "Perhaps you could keep an ear open for something and let me know."

At her side, Lizzie nodded. "But what about the other?"

Mystified, Lydia looked into the other girl's mischievous eyes. "What other?"

"Do you love either of them?"

"Of course not. I hardly know them."

They paused at the door and Lizzie chuckled. "I'm guessing you know them better than most people do."

Lydia shrugged. "Perhaps. I couldn't say."

❧

Lydia stepped to the sidewalk with the paper-wrapped bundle under her arm. *Why haven't either of them married? A wife would certainly solve their need for a housekeeper,* she mused.

Across the street she saw Sam and Matt loading the supplies into the wagon. For a minute she watched them work.

Sam, tall and wiry, moved with a quickness she had come to expect of everything he did. It seemed Sam wasn't about to waste his time at anything. His hat was pushed back and as he swung a box over the side of the wagon she caught a glimpse of his blond hair combed back from his forehead as always. She couldn't see his eyes from where she stood, but she knew the intensity of the blue gaze that seemed to pierce right through a person. She knew he was steady, pleasant, and hardworking.

And Matt? She shifted her gaze to the other man. What did she know about him? His back was to her as he hoisted a five-gallon bucket into the wagon. Even across the distance she could see his back muscles ripple. He was stockier than Sam, more muscular. She'd had a glimpse or two of his arms and knew they were thick as fence posts; she'd seen them bulge when he bent to pick up the bucket of water to add to the boiler on the stove. He had warm brown eyes that could probably melt a young lady's heart with their softness. He had a ready sense of humor that hovered just below the surface. Not as quiet as Sam, he had an easiness about him.

She sighed. *If only they had a Christian faith.*

The creak of an approaching wagon caught Lydia's attention and she stepped back as it passed, wrinkling her nose at the strong smell of sweating horses.

As the wagon passed, Sam glanced up and saw her. Slowly he straightened and murmured something to Matt. Matt turned. They stared for a moment then headed in her direction.

Lydia took a deep breath and waited for them.

"Well, don't you look fine," said Matt as his gaze skimmed her from head to toe.

She smoothed her skirt and ducked her head. "Thank you," she managed, her tongue suddenly thick and cumbersome.

"Nice," Sam murmured his agreement. "Were you able to get the supplies?"

"Oh, yes." She glanced up in time to see how Sam's eyes lingered on her hair. She coughed a little. "Mr. Smith said he'd have it ready for you to load when you came by."

"Great. Thanks." Sam sounded like he had a lump of mud stuck in his throat. He turned to Matt. "Shall we?" And he stepped off the sidewalk and headed for the wagon.

Lydia wondered why Matt chuckled as he started to follow.

"Wait," Lydia implored and both men turned to her. "I didn't. . .that is, I couldn't. . ." She stopped and took a deep breath. "I wasn't able to find another job."

Sam grinned at Matt then said, "Does this mean you're coming back to the ranch with us?"

"If it meets with your approval."

Matt grabbed his hat and slapped it against his thigh as he let out a whoop that made Lydia jump and glance up the street to see how many people heard him. Two ladies coming out of the mercantile looked their way then bent their heads together. "You can count on it!" he roared. "I thought I was going to have to give up homemade bread." He threw his hat in the air. "This calls for a celebration." He turned to Sam. "How would it be if we all have supper at the hotel before we head home?"

Sam, heading for the wagon, called over his shoulder. "Fine with me."

"Would you like that, Lydia?" Matt asked.

"Yes, I would."

"Give us a few minutes to get the supplies, then we'll be ready."

Content to watch the activities of the busy little town, Lydia leaned against a post and waited. As soon as they were loaded, the men tied the wagon in an alley and strode down the sidewalk toward her, their boots thudding against the boards. In their denim jackets and wide-brimmed hats they radiated power and a sense of wildness that was an echo of the land they rode.

Matt hooked his hand around her elbow and escorted her across the street and down the sidewalk to the Empress Hotel. Sam dropped her parcel in the wagon and followed in their trail.

Her steps faltered as they entered the dining room and she stared. Snow-white tablecloths were the background for sparkling china and crystal. Lydia drank in the air of luxury as Matt led her to a table and Sam held the chair for her.

Lydia couldn't shake a nervousness that made her want to turn and run. She was a servant girl. She didn't belong in such surroundings except to fetch and carry. She choked back a giggle thinking how offended some of her former employers would be if they saw her here.

A leather-covered menu was placed in her hands. A sigh escaped her lips and she settled back into her chair. This was an experience to be enjoyed, not questioned, and she glanced at the selection.

What would she choose from so many good things?

Oysters, duck, salmon, or turkey?

Sam turned his blue gaze upon her and she felt her cheeks warm. "Do you see something you'd like?" he asked kindly.

It was a moment before she could answer. "I don't know. It all looks so good but I'm not familiar with many of the dishes."

Matt pushed her menu down so he could see her face. "Are you brave enough to try something completely new?"

She almost choked. "I think so. What do you suggest?"

Matt leaned toward her, pointed to the menu, and made a few suggestions.

She stared at his blunt fingers skimming the items on the menu and caught the scent of grass-covered hills. Her own senses were swept with the feel of a warm prairie breeze.

Only half aware of what he said, she settled for letting him order for her.

In a few minutes they placed their order and as they waited Lydia unfolded the white napkin and placed it on her lap, suddenly so shy she couldn't look up for fear of meeting a pair of blue or brown eyes. She curled her fingers until the nails bit into her palms. Her insides quivered uncertainly. It was all this talk of marriage, she decided. Granny, Alice, and now Lizzie planting thoughts she was trying hard to ignore.

Marriage was, of course, out of the question, yet the remarks had accumulated until she was acutely aware of the two men.

Sam tipped the water jug to fill her glass and smiled slowly.

She nibbled her food but it could have been anything under the sun. For the life of her she couldn't seem to keep her mind on the meal.

Her fork slipped from her hand and landed on the carpet. She bent to retrieve it at the same time as Sam; their fingers brushed as they reached for the utensil. She jerked back, her nerves twitching. *This is ridiculous. Lizzie and her crazy ideas.*

But it wasn't the idea that was crazy. It was her silly response to it. She was so aware of every move the men made that she rattled like a wind-driven pile of junk.

The rest of the meal passed in a fog. Lydia didn't know what she ate or when the dishes where changed. Matt's boisterous chuckle made her jump in alarm and Sam's quieter laugh tickled across her nerves.

They finished their meal and drank their last cup of coffee.

Lydia forced her wooden tongue to speak. "That was wonderful." She folded her napkin and laid it beside her cup. "Thank you."

"It was our pleasure." Matt grinned. "Umm, um. Home-made bread. Hot meals when we get home. Clean clothes. I'd say we got the better end of the stick."

Lydia's face grew hot as she met Matt's eyes. The look in them warmed her insides in a way she didn't understand.

Sam pushed his chair back and moved to hold hers. As she stood she could feel the warmth of him. She breathed the scent of him—a clean, masculine smell of the outdoors. His arm brushed hers as he guided her from the table. Her rib cage tightened. Taking a steadying breath, she murmured her thanks and walked toward the door with legs that were stiff and unreliable.

Both men reached to open the door. Stepping back to make room for them, Lydia bumped into Matt's chest.

"Careful there," he murmured, grabbing her to steady her.

The tips of her ears burned and she realized Sam stood at the door waiting. Barely able to speak, she mumbled her thanks again, praying she wouldn't trip. Never had she felt so awkward.

She'd spent the better part of a fortnight in the presence of these two men. Why should she suddenly be so self-conscious around them?

Matt jumped into the wagon and took the reins while Sam held out his hand to assist her. She rested her hand in his palm and gripped it as she stepped up. Determined to ignore the way her heart lurched at the feel of his strength, she quickly withdrew her hand and sat stiffly on the hard seat. She would face forward all the way home, she decided, and pretend Sam and Matt were strangers.

As they turned toward home the sun tinted the scattered clouds with a golden underlay.

The sky is wearing a gold crown, thought Lydia. *A golden crown for a golden day.*

"Look at that sunset," Sam said. "Looks like the promise of a good day tomorrow."

"Yep," Matt drawled. "We should get a good start on that shed."

The men discussed their plans for the morrow but Lydia didn't listen. Her thoughts were on Sam's words. The promise of a good tomorrow. It had a nice sound to it. Anticipation swelled inside until it caught in her throat. Tomorrow and tomorrow. Life was a bright promise, and she vowed she'd enjoy it fully regardless of all the uncertainties.

As the men's voices rumbled around her she silently spoke to God. *Lord, it's been a good day. There have been times I wondered if You were looking after me; if You truly cared, when all the time You have kept me safe. Help me to trust You for each day.*

five

Supper was quiet that evening. Sam seemed lost in his thoughts. Matt twirled the ends of his mustache and stared into space. Even Granny, after asking about acquaintances in town and reading her handful of letters, lapsed into silence.

Lydia sat up straight. "Alice says they have church in Akasu every Sunday." Her words came out in a breathless rush. "She says I could go with them if I had a ride to their place."

Sam's head jerked up. Matt dropped his chair to all fours and stared at her.

"Would you like to go?" Matt's voice reflected his surprise.

"I have always gone to church on Sunday. It just seems like the right thing to do—to get together with other believers whenever possible."

"Then you shall go." Matt looked toward Sam but Sam stared at the wall behind Lydia. Matt raised his eyebrows briefly then shrugged his shoulders. "I'll take you myself." He tipped back in his chair again and turned his attention to the study of the ceiling. "And I'll take you right to town."

"You don't have to do that," Lydia protested, but when he didn't answer, she murmured, "Thank you."

Later, she finished her bedtime rituals and went to the small desk in front of the window. The silvery moonlight bathed the scene outside in tinsel hues. She took out her Bible from the drawer, opening it to the Psalms. She turned to Psalm 19, recalling how Mother helped her to memorize these verses so many years ago, and she read the first verse, "The heavens declare the glory of God; and the firmament sheweth his handywork."

She stared out the window at the trees and hills bathed in moonlight.

Living here, she had seen so much of the beauty of God's creation. *Thank You, God, for that beauty.*

With a contented sigh, she turned back to the Book and lifted the worn leather of the front cover to the tattered picture of Mother. How she would have enjoyed the beauty. If only Mother were here to offer advice in dealing with her feelings. Since Lizzie's remarks, Lydia hadn't been able to stop thinking about marriage—how it would provide her with a home where she belonged, and someone to love her. *Neither Matt nor Sam is for me, but surely there is someone. . .*

Mother's voice came to her reminding her of God's care. God would lead. God has the answers.

Lydia shut the Bible and closed her eyes. In the quietness of her room, she committed her desires to the Lord.

ﱲ

Sunday morning Lydia put on her new dress and lingered in her room trying to recreate the softer hairdo Lizzie had fashioned. She found she was better at recapturing the enjoyment of the day. At the sound of Matt bringing the wagon to the house, she hurried from her room.

"Everything seems so crystal clear today," she told Matt as they rumbled along the trail. The sky was a flawless blue, the sounds of the birds clear and sweet; the spicy scent of the grass tickled her nose.

"It's one of those rare prairie days when the air is still and pure."

"Of course. There's no wind." She had come to expect the varying levels of it.

The town was muted as they traveled Main Street, every business closed, the sidewalks quiet. And then she saw the steeple of a church.

Matt pulled to a stop in front of the building and jumped down to offer her a hand. Lydia's feet had barely touched the ground when Alice rushed to her side.

"I'm so glad you came." She threw her arms around Lydia in a quick hug. "Come, I'll introduce you before we go in."

Lydia glanced over her shoulder. Matt was already back in the wagon.

"I'll be back to get you." His hat hid his eyes, but his lips formed a firm line under his mustache.

"You aren't coming in?" Alice tugged at her arm but Lydia hung back.

"No." And with a flick of the reins, the wagon rumbled away.

Alice pulled at her arm, but Lydia watched Matt over her shoulder until he turned into the street. Only then did she follow Alice toward a group of people, a heavy lump settling around her heart. She had assumed Matt would accompany her to church.

"This is Mrs. Esther Johnson," Alice said, pausing in front of a woman surrounded by four little girls with large eyes and long black hair. Lydia wondered if the infant in her arms was a boy.

As they edged toward the church, a man joined them.

"Lydia, this is my husband, Norman." Alice looked at him proudly.

Norman had sandy-colored hair and a generous case of freckles; he smiled gently at his wife before he turned to Lydia and held out his hand. "I'm pleased to meet you. Allie has told me much about you."

"We'd better hurry," Alice said, and with Norman on one side and Lydia on the other, drew them through the doors and toward the front of the church.

Lydia settled herself and looked about. To one side of the platform an older lady pumped the organ. Her graying hair bulged out from below a very ugly black hat with a frayed feather swaying in rhythm to her pumping feet. The familiar hymns had a startling quality as the organist struck several wrong notes.

"That's Reverend Arthur Law," whispered Alice, indicating the man seated on the platform. "He came in January. Seems to be a very ambitious young man."

Lydia studied the man. His fair hair dipped in a wave across his forehead. He had a fine, straight nose and a narrow chin with the most appealing dimple right in the center.

"I expect he's set a few hearts fluttering," Alice whispered in her ear.

So that's what you call it, and Lydia attempted to calm the trembling inside her chest as she turned to grin at Alice. "Do you really think so?"

Alice giggled behind her hand.

"Could you open your hymnbooks to number ninety-seven for the opening song?" asked a deep, well-modulated voice.

Reverend Law had taken his place while they whispered and giggled. For some unfathomable reason, it struck Lydia as funny and she lifted the hymnbook to hide her face and hoped he wouldn't be able to see her shaking shoulders.

She lowered her book as Reverend Law raised his rich voice to lead the singing. The words squeaked out of her throat as she tried to join in. She realized she was staring. He was the best-looking, best-sounding man she'd ever encountered.

She hung on his every word as he gave the sermon, uttering familiar words of God's care and all-seeing knowledge, but the sensations racing up and down her spine at the sound of his voice were totally unfamiliar.

Even after he closed in prayer and walked to the back of the church to greet the members of the congregation, Lydia stared at the pulpit. Alice nudged her and giggled.

"Fluttering heart?" she whispered.

Lydia jerked her gaze away and blinked. "Something like that," she mumbled and rose to follow Alice and Norman. At the back, Alice pulled her forward, her eyes twinkling.

"Reverend, I'd like to introduce you to my friend, Lydia Baxter."

He gently took Lydia's hand between both of his. "I noticed you sitting with the Youngs." His warm voice seemed to suggest his notice had been more than ordinary. "I'm very pleased to meet you." He bent closer. "Are you new to the community?"

Alice pushed in. "She's been here a few weeks. She lives at the Twin Spurs."

"Then may I welcome you? And please extend an invitation to the rest of your family."

"But—"

Alice grabbed her arm and pulled her outside, calling over her shoulder, "Thank you, Reverend Law."

Outside, she turned to face Lydia. "That was close."

"What?"

"I don't think the right Reverend Law would consider it proper conduct for you to be keeping house for two bachelors who don't attend church. Even with Granny Arness's critical supervision."

Lydia stared and then narrowed her eyes. "You're right, of course, but how do you suggest I keep it a secret?"

Alice shrugged. "I don't rightly know." She grinned. "I don't suppose we could lie?" And she giggled.

Lydia's jaw dropped and then she laughed. "I wouldn't have imagined you could be so wicked."

Alice tossed her head. "As if I'd really do it." Her smile didn't fade one inch and Lydia knew there was a wide mischievous streak not far below the surface of the efficient Mrs. Young.

Matt pulled the wagon into the yard and Alice gave Lydia a quick hug before Matt helped her to the hard seat. Lydia was still smiling as they headed toward the ranch.

"Looks like you enjoyed yourself."

Lydia wriggled. "I did." Her thoughts lingered overlong on Reverend Law. The unmarried, handsome Reverend Law. She filled her lungs and let her breath out slowly. Was it only last night she had asked God to provide a suitable candidate for marriage?

She turned to look into Matt's face. "I thought you would attend church."

"It wouldn't do me any good. Besides, I can't see any difference between those who go to church and those who don't."

The words stung Lydia. Even though she sometimes harbored doubts about whether or not God cared, she didn't wish to be told she didn't act any differently than some heathen. "God commanded us to meet together." Her lips puckered as she spoke.

"Well, I think the outdoors is a better place to worship than some dark, musty building."

Lydia plucked at a flower in the material of her skirt. His words made her twitch. "Don't you believe in God?" She held her breath, certain that he would admit a deep knowledge of God's love even amidst his doubts—a mirror of her own situation. And if she were honest with herself—she prayed he would reveal the sort of growing faith she hoped to find in the man she married.

"Not a whole lot. I can't see how a loving God would allow awful things like floods that leave people homeless or fevers that kill whole families."

Her body was numb with the hopelessness of his words.

"I learned a long time ago it was safer to believe in myself."

"Was it flood or fever?" she whispered.

"What?" His voice crackled with tension.

"That took your family." It hurt to say the words, but something had happened to his family that left him angry and defensive. And blaming God.

"What makes you think it was that?"

"Your anger." The words fell into a long silence.

His hands clenched on the reins and he stared ahead. Lydia

stole a glance out of the corner of her eye and flinched at the tightness of his jaw. The silence deepened until she could feel it pulsating.

He made a sound like a muffled moan and mumbled, "It was a fever."

"I'm sorry," she whispered, but wondered if he heard her as he continued to speak, his voice rumbling deep in his chest.

"Everyone died but me. Even my baby brother." He stopped as if he could not go on.

"How old were you? What happened to you?"

"I was fourteen. The bank took the farm and I found a job. Been working ever since."

"Matt." She touched his arm. "I'm truly sorry. I know how much it hurts to have no family."

He turned to her and looked deep into her eyes. She couldn't breathe. His expression softened and she remembered she once thought his eyes would have the power to melt a young lady's heart and knew she was correct.

"I guess you would at that." He smiled crookedly, then shrugged. "I learned to live with it a long time ago."

She nodded, her throat too tight for her to speak.

He turned his attention back to the horses. *We share a common pain.* Lydia ached to be able to comfort him even though he made it clear he didn't think he needed it.

If only he would allow God to comfort him.

⁂

Lydia tucked damp strands of hair behind her ears before she bent to open the oven, flinching as the blast of hot air struck her. She sighed her relief. Now that the meat was cooked and the bread baked, she could let the fire die down. She hurried to the open window, fanning her face with her apron. A dust devil skittered across the pathway and fluttered to death in the wilting grass. Heat waves shimmered across the land. But no breeze sighed through the screen.

Only June yet and the heat wave sapped her energy as

much as it parched the land. If only she could do as Granny had and move outdoors to a shady spot.

Wearily, she moved to the other side of the house to look at the lake far below. In the bright sun its hard surface gleamed like a mirror. Matt said when it got hot enough people swam in the water despite the alkali.

I think it's hot enough.

She went to the basin and splashed water on her face before dipping the dishes into the water. She paused frequently to fan her face but she grew hotter by the minute.

Throughout the afternoon the kitchen hoarded the heat, storing it in cupboards to blast in her face when she opened a door, chasing it into corners to throw at Lydia when she picked up a dish. Exhausted, she sank into a chair.

Matt and Sam stomped into the room, faces glistening, shirts damp with sweat.

"It's hotter than an oven out there," said Matt, fanning his hat across his face. "Whew." He gasped. "It's even hotter in here! How do you stand it, Lydia?"

"I try not to think about it. I just keep doing what I have to." Her voice reflected the weakness she felt throughout her body.

Sam paused to call over his shoulder, "Granny, you want something to eat?"

"You won't catch me in that stifling heat. Tell Lydia to bring me something. And some more water."

Sam reached for a milk bottle. "I'll do it." He filled the bottle with water, scooped small portions onto a plate, and carried it outdoors to Granny.

The men ate lightly, explaining it was too hot to eat. Lydia filled the water pitcher three times.

She drooped over her own plate, staring at the food but unable to eat.

Sam shoved his chair back. "We're going to do something about this. Lydia, don't build another fire in the stove. Come on, Matt."

"What do you have in mind?" Matt filled his water glass and drained it before he followed Sam.

"I'll show you."

The screen door rattled shut behind them.

Lydia stared after them a long time before she forced herself to get up and get at her work. As she gathered up dishes, she saw them crossing the yard with armloads of lumber which they piled outside the kitchen window. She poured water from the kettle over the dishes and watched the men pacing out some sort of measurements. The drum of hammers accompanied the swish of her broom.

Finished, she fled outside to escape the heat and sat in the shade a few feet from Granny's rocker watching the men make a frame and nail it into place.

"You'd think those two had enough to do without dreaming up work," Granny said, rocking slowly and fanning herself with a piece of paper. "What are they trying to prove?"

Lydia shrugged.

Soon a shell of a room stood on the grass. Her curiosity stirred. What were they up to?

The shadows lengthened and a gentle breeze drifted across the hills, thinning the heat as the men continued to work.

Granny pushed to her feet and shuffled to the house mumbling, "As if the heat isn't bad enough, how's a body supposed to sleep with all that racket?"

The sweet fragrance of wild roses perfumed the air and Lydia reached over and plucked one of the flat, waxen blossoms from a bush growing tenaciously along the edge of the house. As the evening shadows lengthened, the men continued to pound and saw, the fresh wood smell mingling with the scent of roses.

"We'll have to quit now," Matt called, throwing his hammer on a pile of wood scraps. "We'll finish it in the morning then I'll go to town."

"It should only take a couple more hours." Sam stood back

and surveyed the shell, its roof sloping one direction, its walls naked uprights. "I hope a wind doesn't come up in the night and take our roof off."

Matt removed his hat to mop his brow with his shirt sleeve. "If I hear the wind during the night, I'll get you up and you can sleep on the roof."

"But if you went to sleep on the roof right now, you wouldn't have to worry," Sam replied.

Matt swung his hat at him. Sam ducked and pretended to throw a punch at Matt.

How can they find the energy? Lydia wondered as she dragged herself to her feet and went to her bedroom.

Despite her exhaustion, she tossed and turned, unable to find relief from the heat.

Dawn brought a blast of already overheated air. Lydia lay staring through her window at the brassy sky. She was tired and her head still ached. She tossed aside the sheet and struggled out of bed, pulling her nightie away from her sticky body. She straightened the bed covers before pulling on a worn cotton dress, the coolest thing she had. Already weary, she sank into the chair, pulling her Bible toward her. It fell open at the crocheted bookmark Mrs. Williams had made for her when she first began to work for them.

She wondered how Annabelle was doing as a nanny and whether Gracie and the other children missed Lydia. Then she read a few verses. But her foggy mind refused to concentrate. Finally, she closed the Bible in defeat and let her head fall into her arms.

Lord, I can't take this heat. I'm so tired I feel sick. Please, could You send some cooler weather? And give me strength to make it through today.

She heard Sam and Matt cross the kitchen and the screen door slap shut. Almost at once she heard them hammering outside her window.

I suppose they want to work before it gets any hotter.

Though if it gets any hotter I'm sure to melt into a little pool of butter right in front of the stove.

Then she remembered Sam told her not to light another fire in it.

I don't know how I'll make them their porridge or heat water to wash dishes. She dragged herself to the kitchen, took out bread, sliced it, and set out butter and jam.

The rose blossom lay on the table where she'd dropped it last night. It was still fragrant but shriveled and ugly. For a moment she looked at it, wishing she could put it in water and restore it, yet knowing it was beyond help. She felt a sharp pain at the destroying power of the heat.

She called the men. They hurried in and quickly spread generous amounts of butter and jam on thick slices of bread.

Watching them gave her a queasy feeling.

"I think you can finish by yourself," Matt said to Sam as he tipped his chair back. "I'll go into town and get the things we need."

Sam nodded. "I'll get at it before it gets any hotter out there." The men rose and left. Lydia heard the rattle of the wagon as it left the yard and then more hammering.

With little work to do in the kitchen, she went outside.

Half the building had walls right to the ceiling; the other half had waist-high walls. Sam nailed a ledge on top of one of the shorter walls.

"Come over here and I'll show you what we've done," he called.

Lydia did so.

"The stove will go here," said Sam pointing at the tallest of the walls. "These walls will allow the heat to escape and any breeze to blow through." He pointed at the partial walls. "We'll build some shelves and a table for you. Then you will be able to cook without heating the house up."

She turned full circle, admiring the construction. They had thought of everything. Sam beamed as she smiled and nodded.

She turned her eyes toward him, letting his piercing blue gaze reach into her mind. Today he seemed tall and comforting and thoughtful.

"What a good idea! Thank you for thinking of it." She forced the words past a tongue that had grown stiff.

"I'm sorry and ashamed we didn't think of it sooner. Most farms have a summer kitchen, but we were too busy with our own concerns to think about how hot the kitchen gets in a heat spell like this." The color in his eyes deepened as he shifted his stance and crossed his arms. He seemed reluctant to tear his gaze away and she couldn't find the strength to do so. As they looked deeply into each other's eyes, something warm and golden began to swell behind her heart and she found it difficult to breathe.

"I sure hope this doesn't build into a hailstorm," Sam murmured.

Lydia blinked and filled her lungs. With limbs that felt borrowed, she crossed to one of the open walls where she strove to pull her thoughts into order. Any form of relief from the heat would be welcome, but then she corrected herself, knowing how devastating a storm could be.

She looked into the overly bright sky wondering if the blue of Sam's eyes was embedded in her brain. Thinking of the way he'd looked at her, she grew even warmer.

"Come, I want to show you something." Sam took her hand and led her out of the summer kitchen and away from the house.

The heat rushing up her body was suffocating. "Where are we going, Sam?"

"Just over that little hill." He pointed to the rise north of them.

Hand in hand they crossed the yellowed grass, kicking up dust. *We're kicking up more than dust,* Lydia thought as shivers raced through her stomach.

A brown bird with a long, curved beak flew around them calling, "Pivot, pivot."

"What kind of bird is that?" she asked, hoping conversation would calm her nerves, knowing that nothing but dropping his hand would do so. Yet he showed no sign of releasing their grasp.

"Most people call him a curlew. He's trying to chase us away. Probably has young ones nearby."

A second and then a third bird joined the first, circling and squawking. Then a fourth bird came.

"It sounds like he's got a cold," Lydia said as the bird flew around them. They stopped to listen, laughing at the raspy voice. As Sam lowered his eyes, a shaft of sunlight flashed across his face and lit his eyes with an intensity that made Lydia gasp. For a heartbeat she thought her chest would explode.

It's only the enjoyment of a shared moment, she told herself, forcing calmness to return. *Simple pleasure in a simple thing.*

Sam led her to the top of the hill. "Look below you," he said.

"Oh," Lydia gasped, "it's beautiful!"

The bottom of the hill was a mass of orange flowers so vivid she could hardly believe they were real. She picked up her skirts and, momentarily forgetting the heat, ran the last few yards to kneel among the cup-shaped orange stars. Sam squatted down on his heels next to her, his eyes on her face as she tenderly touched the blossoms.

She raised her face to him. "Oh, Sam, they're like china teacups. What are they called?"

His expression was gentle. "They're wild tiger lilies," he said softly, his low voice swelling in her mind until— She gulped. "Is it all right if I pick some?"

Sam pulled out his pocketknife. "Here, let me. They have tough stems." He handed her the handful of blooms. Their hands touched. A shock ran through Lydia's body.

They stood. She raised her eyes to his. They were inches

apart, both clasping the bouquet. Lydia's heart refused to function. She held her breath, aware of the intensity of his blue eyes, then he dropped his arm and turned away, shoving his hands into the back pockets of his pants.

"We better be getting back," he said. "I need to finish up the summer kitchen before Matt returns."

Lydia inhaled the subtle fragrance of the tiger lilies.

Sam strode up the hill as if his pants were on fire. Sweat poured down Lydia's face as she struggled to keep up. At the top, he stopped and turned, waiting for her. As soon as she caught her breath she said, "Thank you for the flowers, Sam."

He smiled. "You're welcome. I thought you would enjoy them."

Lydia nodded then hurried toward the house.

Granny had watched them the whole time. "Don't let a few flowers make a fool of you."

Lydia bit back the sharp retort that sprang to her lips and rushed inside to find a container. Granny's words burned in her mind as she lingered over arranging the flowers. *No, I won't let a few flowers, or even a few warm glances, sway me from my decision to wait for the right man—the man God will provide—before I fall in love.*

She made sandwiches. They were on a plate covered with a clean tea towel when Matt drove into the yard and over to the summer kitchen. The men unloaded a new stove and pipes. In a few minutes they had the stove set up and the pipes running through the wall. Matt gathered kindling and coal while Sam wiped the stove off. They lit a fire and stood back. As soon as they were certain it was working well, Matt drove the wagon up to the door of the house.

"It's all ready to go," he announced, carrying a large box to the table. "Wait until you see what else I got."

Sam followed him, each carrying a box.

"The Johnsons, from south of town, were there. They'd picked saskatoon berries and brought them to town to sell, so

I got some." He indicated two of the boxes full of small purple berries mixed with leaves and twigs. Two more boxes contained jars.

Matt proudly stated, "I thought you could can them and we could have fruit this winter. I just love fruit of any kind. I expect there will be peaches in pretty soon, too. We got that summer kitchen built just in time."

Lydia stared at the fruit and the jars. She understood she was expected to can them, but how did one can fruit? She dropped to a chair and gaped at the boxes on the table.

She was aware of Sam watching her.

"I guess I'll put the horses away before I eat." Matt left.

Sam twisted his hat in his hands. Finally he spoke. "Lydia, are you all right?"

She raised her head but his face wouldn't focus and she dropped her gaze back to the box of berries.

"Lydia, what's the matter?" Sam persisted. He followed her eyes to the berries. "Don't you know how to can?"

She shook her head.

He turned to Granny. "I suppose you know what to do?"

Granny snorted. "Young man, if you'll stop and think, you'll recall I said from the outset that I was too old and crippled to do heavy work." She picked up her knitting as if to dismiss the whole idea. "Lydia will have to learn on her own just like I had to at her age."

six

Lydia lifted her head and watched Sam.

His eyes darkened and his mouth drew to a hard line as he glowered at the older woman. Turning on his heel, he mumbled something under his breath then filled the kettle and took it out to the summer kitchen.

Lydia picked up a jar, examining it closely, hoping for a clue. Desperate for help, she determined to beg Granny to tell her the essentials, but Granny scurried into her bedroom mumbling something about needing a rest.

Sam returned with a pot of tea. "Leave the berries for now. I'll get Alice to come. She'll be able to show you what to do." He poured a cupful and handed it to her.

She swallowed the lump in her throat. "Thank you, Sam." Her voice wobbled noticeably. After he left she got the recipe book Alice had lent her and hunched over the pages but could not find any instructions for canning fruit. It must be something a person was supposed to know, maybe learning it from her mother.

Mrs. Williams's cook had done up jars of fruit and pickles and vegetables. Lydia squeezed her eyes tightly trying to recall if she'd seen how it was done, but all she recalled was the steamy kitchen, the way her nose twitched from the smell of simmering vinegar, and rows of jars cooling on the table. Cook had not allowed anyone to linger when she was busy.

She paged through the recipe book again. It yielded no more information the second time through. Nor the third.

Lydia stood and stared into the box of berries then leaned over the box of jars and blinked. Did she expect to get inspiration from their contents? She took out a jar turned it round and round and shook it. She exhaled sharply. One would think instructions would be included. She took out each jar and examined the interior of the box. The only words she could find were the name on the sealers.

She paced the room then fled to the summer kitchen where she ran her fingers over the ledges and the square wooden table, white and pure. Nothing yielded any information.

Desperate, she hurried back indoors, not slowing until she stood in the doorway of Granny's room.

But Granny lay with her back to the room, snoring softly. Lydia didn't know if the old lady was asleep or pretending, but it was obvious she didn't intend to help.

With heavy steps, Lydia returned to the kitchen and plunked down on a chair.

A suffocating sense of despair had gripped Lydia by the shoulders when the screen door squawked open.

"Well, what do we have here?"

Lydia sagged with relief at the sound of Alice's voice.

"Am I glad to see you! I hope you can tell me what I'm supposed to do with these saskatoons."

"That's why I'm here." Alice crossed to the table and peered in the boxes. "Sam told me you needed some help. I'm an old hand at this sort of thing. I've helped my mother since I was old enough to carry a pail of water."

"Thank goodness. You'll have to tell me everything. I've never done this before."

"First, let's take it all out to the summer kitchen. By the way, when did the boys build that?"

"They finished it this morning. Fact is, I haven't used it yet."

They carried out the boxes of fruit, the cases of jars and lids, buckets of water, and the pots and pans, while Alice kept up a steady stream of instructions.

Lydia strained to remember it all, hoping it would make more sense once she'd done some of it.

"There, that's the first batch ready," said Alice a few hours later as she lowered a jar of purple fruit into the boiler of hot water. "We'll sort some more berries while they boil."

Lydia sank to a chair by the plank table, the new white wood now stained with saskatoon juice. She scooped some berries into her bowl and proceeded to pick out the leaves and twigs as she listened to Alice's chatter.

"This heat has sure been hard on my garden. I don't know how many more days it can take before it dies. I've been giving it as much water as I can spare but I don't know. . . I remember one year Mother. . ."

Her voice faded as Lydia concentrated her energies on the tedious job of removing debris from the berries. Canning was a chore she wouldn't classify as easy work.

"We'll take these jars out now and set them to cool."

As Alice hurried to the stove, Lydia's head jerked up. Lost in her thoughts, she'd heard nothing of what Alice said.

"I'll help you get the next batch in, then I'll have to get home. It looks like there might be a storm coming up."

Lydia looked up. Far to the west she saw a white-tipped, dark cloud churning. But the air drifting through the little shack was still oven hot.

A little later, Alice gathered her things and tied a bonnet over her flyaway blond hair. She paused. "I hate to leave you to finish this alone." She cast an anxious eye at the sky.

"I'll be fine. You get on home and thanks so much for your help." Lydia remained seated, sorting berries, pausing only to wave good-bye and call her thanks.

"Anytime," Alice called. She hesitated a moment more then climbed into the wagon and rattled away.

As Lydia turned back to her task, a refreshingly cool breeze rippled across her neck, teasing her damp hair.

Cook the berries in the syrup, pour them into the jars, screw the lids down—not too tightly—and carefully lower them into the boiling water. Lydia repeated each instruction as she finished up the last of the saskatoons. *Now wash up the dishes, throw out the garbage, and put everything away.*

A blast of wind rattled the walls. Lydia looked up to a black, foaming sky. She shook her head, letting the cool air sweep her neck. Then she quickly covered the hot jars, making a dash to the house for more tea towels.

"You'd do well to hurry up," Granny said as Lydia raced into the kitchen. "I can't imagine what's taking you so long. Why, I remember when I did two hundred jars or more on my own."

Lydia paused, her hands full of towels, and stared at the older woman. "I'm sure you did." Her voice was strained. She took a deep breath to calm herself. "But don't worry. I'm just about done."

Granny's eyes widened and her mouth dropped open, but Lydia hurried from the room without waiting for a reply. She shook her head. She shouldn't let Granny's comments get to her. After all, the old lady was in pain and alone in the world despite Lydia's attempts to befriend her.

Lydia lifted the jars from the hot water and carefully arranged them on a piece of wood on the floor, hoping it would be enough protection from the cool breeze. Alice had warned her the hot jars wouldn't seal if they were bumped or cooled too quickly.

Lightning flashed across the sky and thunder rumbled over the hills as Lydia prepared supper then carried it indoors.

As the men crossed the yard, she heard them discussing the storm, wondering if it would bring hail or rain.

Sam paused at the door. "Did you get the saskatoons done?" The gentleness in his voice made her eyes sting.

"Yes, I've just finished."

"How many jars did you get?" Matt's voice was muffled by the towel as he dried his face.

"I think it was forty jars."

"Good job," Matt said, looking pleased. "It will be great

having fruit next winter."

"You did great," Sam added. "But it was a lot of work." He looked at her closely. "You look tired."

His concern and the expression in his eyes lifted her fatigue. Suddenly she felt like singing. She smiled at him, "I'm fine."

It didn't rain or hail but the heat ended. The following days were more tolerable and Lydia breathed a sigh of relief.

"It's early," Matt warned. "We could see lots of hot weather yet."

But Lydia didn't care as long as it remained bearable for the time being.

❧

Sunday morning broke with a cloudless sky, a gentle breeze promising moderate temperatures. Lydia fussed over her hair wanting to look her best for church.

Sunday after Sunday Reverend Law asked about her well-being. Lydia liked to hope his interest and the way he looked at her with such a kind smile meant he was developing something more than pastorly interest.

She tucked in a strand of hair and studied herself in the mirror. She was being foolish. Reverend Law had been nothing but a perfect gentleman. There was no reason to pin her hopes in that direction. No reason—except for Alice's constant remarks.

"He's smitten with you," Alice had whispered as they parted a few Sundays ago.

"Me?" She wished Alice was right.

Alice leaned closer. "He'd have to be blind not to have taken notice of you as more than another warm body in the pew. Blind and a little deficient." She winked at Lydia. "And we know he's neither."

The way she waggled her eyebrows made Lydia giggle. "There's no reason for him to notice."

Her expression gentle, Alice grabbed Lydia's arm and

walked her to the wagon where Matt sat waiting. "Don't sell yourself short," she ordered.

Matt waited until Lydia was seated before he asked, "Sell yourself short at what?"

Lydia almost choked, thinking how Matt would react to the truth. The idea made her giggle.

"Now you have to tell me."

She turned to see his lips twitching under a mustache that wiggled like something alive. It made her laugh harder so she couldn't speak. He shook his head but as he drove from the yard he growled, "Are you going to tell me what's so funny or do I have to squeeze it out of you?"

His words interrupted her laughter; her mouth was suddenly as parched as the prairie grass. She stammered, "Alice th-thinks I'm too hard on myself."

He slanted a look at her. "Could be she's right." He paused. "You're an interesting young woman."

She'd stared at the horse's ears trying to think what he meant. *Interesting? In a good way or a strange way?*

❧

The next week, as soon as the last elderly couple had shaken hands with the pastor, Reverend Law hurried down the steps toward the small group where Lydia stood.

Alice winked at Lydia, sending Lydia's thoughts into confusion.

Reverend Law paused at Lydia's side. "Would you care to stroll around the yard?"

Lydia glanced toward the street. Matt had not arrived yet. She had a few moments to enjoy a stroll. "I'd like that."

"How are you finding your new home?" Reverend Law bent closer, making her feel like he couldn't wait for her answer. His dark blue eyes were gentle and she lowered her lashes before she answered.

"I enjoy the beauty of the prairies. I only wish. . ." She paused, thinking how much Mother would have enjoyed the details of color and texture and movement.

"Wish what?"

"I wish my mother could see it." Her throat was so tight she could barely speak.

"Is your mother back in England?"

She had told him very little about herself. "My mother passed away a few years ago."

"I'm so sorry."

She was sure Mother would approve of Reverend Law. He was so refined, so cultured, so handsome.

"How are you doing otherwise?"

Her thoughts had run away. "I'm sorry. I'm not sure what you mean."

"I like to pray for you during the week and wondered if there was anything special I could pray for."

She lifted her face to him then and met his eyes, feeling as if she soared, so great was her joy. No one had offered to pray for her since Mother had died.

Afterward, she couldn't remember her answer. All she could remember was how she'd seen him as if for the first time. A glowing light seemed to radiate from him.

That was a week ago and as she prepared for church now, her hand trembled at the thought of seeing him again. It had taken several tries before she got her hair pinned in place—just in time, for she heard the wagon and hurried from the house to join Matt. There was only one dark spot in her day—despite her asking him repeatedly to attend the meeting with her, Matt continued to drop her at the church door and drive away. And Sam refused every invitation to accompany them.

When the final "amen" was said, Lydia turned to Alice. "It was a lovely sermon."

Alice laughed. "And what was it about?"

Lydia gave a toss of her head. "God and love and Jesus."

Her friend giggled. "I'm sure it was love you were thinking about."

"Was not. You're way off." She'd been thinking about the way Reverend Law's hair seemed to catch the rays of sunlight. She'd been wondering if he would draw her aside again.

But when she got to where he stood, a family clustered around him talking earnestly. She hurried outside, swallowing her disappointment.

The family must have had a lot to discuss because the parishioners left one by one until Lydia was alone in the yard. She had stared down the road for ages waiting for Matt, but there was no sign of him.

The door behind her clicked shut and she turned. Reverend Law stared at her. "I thought you would have left by now," he said. "Where is your brother? Why hasn't he come for you?"

"He isn't. . .I don't. . .I don't know what has become of him." At first, she'd welcomed Matt's delay, hoping it would give her a chance to see the pastor again, but now she was really and truly concerned.

Reverend Law hurried down the steps to her side.

"Where does he usually go while he waits?"

"I. . .I don't know." She'd never asked.

Reverend Law pulled his watch from his pocket and studied it. "I'm sure he'll be here soon. In the meantime, why don't we sit down and relax?"

She should have welcomed the extra time, but she could feel trembles starting in her legs. What could possibly have happened to Matt? She envisioned the wagon overturned and Matt injured.

Finally, the pastor checked his watch again. "I think I'd better get a buggy and take you home. Perhaps your brother has forgotten you."

She shook her head. Matt wouldn't do that. But she didn't bother to say so. Somehow it was more important to find a way to set him straight about Matt being her brother.

Before she could decide the best way to say it, he rose.

"Perhaps you should wait inside until I'm ready to go."

"Of course." The building seemed dark and moody with no other occupant, and shivering, she huddled on the edge of a pew.

At the squeak of the door, she jumped to her feet.

"I didn't see any sign of your brother in town," said Reverend Law as he escorted her outside and helped her to the seat of the rented buggy.

"He's not my brother." But he seemed not to hear as he pulled himself up beside her.

"You'll have to direct me as I have never been to the Twin Spurs Ranch."

Lydia indicated the direction. "I can't imagine what has happened to him." She twisted her hands.

"Not to worry. I'm sure there's a reasonable explanation. Now tell me about the ranch."

Grateful for his attempt to divert her concern, she said, "It sits in the hills looking down over the lake with the most wonderful colors that can be rich and vibrant one day and muted the next, depending on the weather."

"It sounds like you're very fond of the place."

"I guess I am." She hadn't thought of it before, but there was something about the ranch that made it special. It almost felt like home. "Tell me about yourself," she said.

"I was born in eastern Canada and came west with my folks when I was almost grown. I'm a graduate of the University of Alberta and of Alberta College where I got my degree in theology."

Lydia was impressed. Such a well-educated man. "Your family must be very proud of you." Her voice revealed her awe.

"My family has always encouraged me."

"Where do they live? How many brothers and sisters do you have?"

"My family still lives in Edmonton, or at least my parents and my youngest brother do. My older brother is a lawyer and my sister is a teacher."

He turned to Lydia. "Is there just you and your brother in your family?"

She studied her hands grasped tightly in her lap. Things were going from bad to worse, but she had no choice but to answer him honestly.

"Matt's not my brother," she whispered, not daring to look up.

"Your cousin then?"

"No. . .no, he's no relation," she blurted.

"I don't understand."

Lydia sighed. He might as well know the truth. Surely he'd understand. "You see, I was employed by Reverend Williams to help his wife care for their children. That's how I came to Canada. But then Annabelle, their niece, wanted my job. I had to find another position, or rather, Reverend Williams found it for me. I thought I was coming to care for a family. It wasn't until I got here I discovered I was going to be housekeeper for two bachelors. I told them it was an impossible situation so they got Granny Arness to move in with us." She thought she'd said it rather well and held her breath waiting for his reaction.

"Two!" His voice was sharp.

Her shoulders drooped. She'd forgotten he didn't know about Sam.

"Yes, there's Sam as well."

His fine eyebrows drew together.

"I've tried to find something else." Her spine seemed to have lost the ability to support her body and she slumped over her knees. "There doesn't seem to be anything."

"Why, Miss Baxter. What an intolerable position."

"They've treated me kindly. And don't forget Granny is there. She's a very capable chaperon." Sam or Matt would have smiled at that. Granny was everything any parent could ask for in that capacity—sharp-eyed, suspicious, and critical.

"Would you like me to see what I can find for you?"

She nodded, unable to speak around the lump in the back of her throat. His voice was so gentle, his concern so evident. She indicated the trail to the ranch house.

As they approached the house, Reverend Law patted her hand. "Now don't you worry about it anymore. I'll find you something."

Lydia stared straight ahead. Was it possible he could find her a new job when no one else had been able to come up with anything? But maybe he was thinking of something different. A pulse thudded under her jaw. There was one position she would jump to have—that of his wife. Could that be what he was hinting at? But he said nothing more as they neared the house.

Sam was at the corrals cleaning a saddle when the buggy entered the yard. He looked up at the sound and when he saw it wasn't Matt escorting Lydia, he vaulted the corral fence and strode across the yard.

"Where's Matt? What's happened?" he demanded.

"I don't know," Lydia murmured, her thoughts in too much turmoil to do more than stare at him.

Sam's eyes narrowed as he watched her, blazing as he turned them on the man beside her.

The reverend jumped down from the wagon and came around to help Lydia, but Sam had already reached up.

Reverend Law faced Sam. "You must be Sam," he said. "I am Reverend Arthur Law." He drew himself up to his full height but still had to look up to meet Sam's eyes.

He took Lydia's arm and escorted her to the house, promising, "I will see you very soon," before he closed the door between them.

seven

Lydia fell against the door, her legs too weak to hold her. The buggy rolled out of the yard. She waited, wondering if Sam would come to the house. After a few minutes she realized he had gone back to work and she straightened. Crumbs indicated Sam had been in to make himself a sandwich. She should eat something as well, but she had no appetite and simply stared at the top of the table.

Granny, moaning, hobbled from her room. "Well, what kept you so long? You'd think a good Christian could get home in time to look after her work."

Lydia clamped her mouth shut and remained quiet.

"What does a body have to do to get fed around here?" Granny plunked down in her chair and glowered at Lydia.

Lydia sighed. There was no point in responding to Granny's comments. "Would you like a sandwich and some tea?"

"Certainly I would."

As Lydia worked, hurt edged her thoughts. How could Matt forget her so easily? Though perhaps she should count it as a blessing, seeing as it provided the opportunity for her to enjoy a buggy ride with Reverend Law. His promise to help her seemed to carry a special meaning.

She put Granny's lunch before her and hurried outdoors to the edge of the hill and, gathering her skirt around her legs, plunked down on the grass.

In the background she heard Sam moving about in the barn and wondered if he waited for Matt's return with the same mix of emotions she felt. But then he was more familiar with Matt's habits and perhaps didn't find this unusual.

It stung to think Matt would treat her this way. She clenched her hands around her knees. Just when she thought things were going well, something went wrong. It seemed to be the story of her life. She longed to bury her head in Mother's lap and let her calm voice guide her. There was no one else she could turn to for comfort and advice.

God, You are the one I must depend on.

For a long time she sat huddled over her knees staring at the lake until the scents and sounds of nature seeped into her thoughts and she began to relax.

The sound of a wagon brought her stumbling to her feet. Her legs had gone to sleep and it was a few minutes before she could walk. By the time she crested the hill she saw Sam facing Matt, shoulders squared, his fists clenched.

She couldn't hear Sam's words but she understood Matt's reply.

"I had something I had to do. It took longer than I thought." He turned to walk away. Sam grabbed his arm and jerked him around.

"You left her at the mercy of every Tom, Dick, and Harry in town." His voice rang across the yard.

Lydia had intended to confront Matt herself, but at Sam's angry words she drew to a standstill.

"The preacher man said he'd taken her home." Matt rolled on the balls of his feet.

"That all he said?"

Matt shrugged. "Nope, but I didn't pay much mind to the rest of it."

Sam glowered at Matt and snorted. "He intends to find a more suitable job for Lydia."

"I wish him the best of luck." He paused to rock back on his heels. "You know he'll be scraping the barrel to find anything." He stretched. "And if he finds anything better, she'd be foolish not to go."

Sam's shoulders relaxed. "Yeah, I suppose so." Then he stiffened again. "Where the scratch were you?"

Matt shrugged and turned away to unhitch the horse. "Just something I had to look after."

Sam stared after him a moment then stomped away.

Lydia waited and when no one noticed her standing at the crest of the hill, hurried toward the house. Too confused to face either of them, she hoped she could slip by without being noticed. When Matt called her name, her heart sank. Slowly, she turned to face him.

He strode over and looked down in her face. "I didn't mean to leave you like that." He lifted his hands. "I plumb forgot the time." His brown eyes begged for understanding.

"Of course," she murmured, dipping her head.

He waited but there didn't seem to be anything more she could say.

"Fine then," he said at last.

She headed toward the house, her heart heavy with disappointment. She couldn't so easily dismiss the knowledge that he'd forgotten all about her.

Granny sat knitting in her rocker. "I see the scallywag decided to return. He was up to no good, you mark my words." She rocked harder. "So he left you to your own resources to find a way home?" When Lydia didn't answer, Granny continued. "I expect you found a substitute easily enough."

Lydia kept her back to Granny and stared out the window. Granny made it sound like Lydia had done something wrong. She blinked back tears. Had everyone turned against her?

She mixed up johnnycake, shoved it in the oven in the summer kitchen, then returned to the house where she sat down to wait for the men to come for supper.

Matt entered first and threw his hat at the hook where it swung for a few seconds then settled. He draped his vest beside it before he bent over the basin. He was scrubbing his hands when the door opened and Sam came in.

Sam took his time hanging his hat and tugging off his boots

then sat and waited for Matt to finish.

Matt looked over the top of the towel as he scrubbed his face dry. "Still mad?" he asked Sam.

Sam drew himself up. "I am not mad."

"Right, and I'm the preacher's wife." Matt flicked the towel at him.

Sam yanked it from his hands then marched past to plunge his hands into the water.

"It won't happen again," Matt promised.

"No, it won't," Sam muttered, drying his hands and face and bunching the towel over the hook.

By the time supper was over, the men were laughing and joking again but the whole business stuck in Lydia's gut. *They are no different from Reverend and Mrs. Williams and all the others before them, forgetting me as easily as one forgets yesterday's yawn. A person should be important enough to be remembered!*

She took her hurt and confusion to bed with her, tossing all night as she turned her thoughts over and over, telling herself it didn't matter what anyone thought. Not Sam or Matt or Reverend Law. Certainly not Granny. God had not and would not abandon her. She would trust Him and Him alone.

Next morning, she looked at herself in the mirror and saw her eyes red-rimmed, her complexion wan.

That's what comes of thinking of yourself more highly than you should. She had to live with what she was—a servant girl with no home of her own.

A quick breakfast soon had the men outside working. Lydia turned to her own chores. Several times she looked out the window to see why the sun felt so cold. Even the color of the trees and flowers had faded.

Granny ventured out of her room, mumbling something about the pain in her back, waiting only long enough for Lydia to refill her hot water bottle and make a pot of tea before she returned to her bed.

By dinnertime the darkness in her heart had not lifted and Lydia served the meal with limbs that seemed heavy. The men said little, though she noticed the look they exchanged before they quietly rose and left the house. She turned back to the table to clear it and stopped like she'd been lassoed. In the center of the table lay a bouquet of wildflowers. There were brown-eyed Susans, harebells, and others she couldn't name. And loads of wild roses. Gingerly she scooped them up, avoiding the thorns on the roses, letting the sweet scent wash through her. A ray of sunlight gleamed through the window and caught the water jug, spraying a burst of color across the table.

Lydia held the flowers to her face for a long time before arranging them in a pitcher. Even then her fingers lingered at the blossoms. The men had cared enough to try to cheer her up. Her heart sang so she could hardly contain it. Her feet skipped across the floor as she did her afternoon chores.

&

Five days later Lydia heard the rumble of an approaching wagon and hurried to the window.

Reverend Law sat upright on the seat.

She'd thought it might be Alice. In fact, she'd wondered if she would see the reverend again before Sunday. She assumed he'd been no more successful at finding her something than she had.

Realizing she was rumpled, she pulled off her apron and patted her hair.

The wagon stopped. She waited for his knock before she opened the door. "Reverend Law, what a pleasant surprise. Do come in." Her heart fluttered like a trapped butterfly.

"Good afternoon. I'm glad to see you're at home. I have good news." He glanced around the room. "It appears you are alone so I will remain here to speak to you." He stood with the door open. Lydia opened her mouth and shut it again, her heart racing too hard to be able to speak. It was almost more than she could do to keep from throwing herself into his arms saying, "Yes, yes, yes! I'll marry you!"

"I have found you a new job." He beamed. "It's with Karl Laartz and his family. They have five young ones and his wife could use some help." He paused and leaned forward, waiting for Lydia's response, but all she could manage was a nod as her limbs wilted.

"The Laartz family lives about fifteen miles south of town," Arthur continued, unaware Lydia was finding it difficult to remain on her feet. "I'm afraid they won't be able to pay you very much—just room and board. And you'll have to share the room where the children sleep. Maybe you can help them learn English at the same time." He finally stopped talking and looked at her. "I know you're surprised I found you something. But where there's a will there's a way." He grabbed the doorknob. "I'll wait out here while you get your things ready."

He walked to the wagon and leaned against it.

Lydia closed the door softly and fell against it, staring across the room. A job looking after a bunch of youngsters who didn't even speak English. It was hardly a proposal of marriage. She struggled to catch her breath.

And yet, wasn't it what she wanted? A job with a family?

She pushed herself away from the door. There was much to do.

In her room she took her valise from the wardrobe and placed it on her bed. She looked about trying to decide where to begin. Moving to the desk, she took her Bible from the drawer and stood holding it. Suddenly her eyes focused. She sank down on the bed, the Bible in her lap.

I asked for a way out, and now I have it. God, You've answered my prayer when I didn't believe You would.

With renewed purpose, she pulled out her trunk and folded her belongings into it then rose and glanced about the pleasant room with the large comfortable bed, a desk under the window that seemed to invite her to sit and enjoy reading or writing, and—she turned full circle—complete privacy.

But it was time to move on. God had provided a way.

She grabbed her packed valise and walked out of the room to grind to a halt in the living room.

She'd cleaned and polished every piece of furniture. The desk Sam brought from England was over a hundred years old. For hours, she'd labored over it with rags and lemon oil until it reflected her face like a mirror. She scanned the objects hanging on the wall then stiffened her back and walked into the kitchen.

A possessive feeling tightened inside her. She'd brought order to this house. She had given it its sparkle. How could she bear to leave knowing the disrepair that would soon sweep over it? Her eyes settled on the bright bouquet that had replaced the one the men left a few days ago, and she dropped her valise, hurrying over to bury her face in the flowers.

Would she find another view like the one from the top of the hill? Would she have time to admire flowers or pick them?

Matt and Sam. How could she leave them? She'd been so afraid of them at first. But now she looked forward to Matt's ready smile and the way he told her the names of the flowers.

And Sam. Sam was quiet and always kind. He offered encouragement with a soft word or two.

Even Granny. What would happen to Granny if she left? The men wouldn't be around to fill her hot water bottle or make her tea in the middle of the morning. And she had no other place to go. How would she manage?

They needed her. They all needed her.

What had Reverend Law said? She would have to share a room with five children! And teach them English! She would be crowded into a corner without any privacy or space and yet—she shuddered—she would be so alone. It would have been different if he had even hinted at marriage. But he'd said nothing.

Lydia lifted her head. Her eyes felt hollow. *I got what I prayed for, but maybe. . .* She hesitated. *Maybe. . .* She drew a deep breath and closed her eyes. *Maybe, what I asked for is not what I need. Or want.*

She squared her shoulders, picked up her valise, and marched into her room to drop it on the bed. With fingers that moved with firm purpose, she pulled out her Bible and returned it to the drawer in the desk.

With growing conviction that she knew what she wanted and where she wanted to be, she headed for the door and threw it open. Only one thing would change her mind. And that was up to Reverend Law.

He looked up as she stood in the doorway. "Are you ready?"

Lydia faced him squarely. "I've decided I'm not going." She met his eyes without blinking. If he had any interest in her as a woman, this was the time to proclaim it.

His mouth dropped and he gathered himself up. "You've what?"

"I've decided I'm not going. At least not to the Laartz's." Would he understand her meaning? She waited. *Give me a better offer and I'll jump at the chance.* But he simply stared at her.

"Lydia, you can't be serious. You're alone here with two unmarried men. Think how it looks. Your reputation will be ruined."

"I'm very serious. Besides, you keep forgetting Granny." She stiffened her spine. Perhaps she had imagined that his kindly interest meant more than it did. "I have a pleasant home here and I have a job to do. I'm going to stay and do it."

"Lydia, you're making a big mistake."

"I'm sorry you came all the way out here for nothing, but I'm not leaving." She blinked hard, determined her eyes would not glisten with tears. If only he would say something that gave her reason to hope he had plans for the future.

A frown drove deep creases into his cheeks. "As your pastor

I must warn you that this is a foolish and dangerous choice you're making."

Unable to speak, she swallowed back the deep, empty feeling.

Finally he turned on his heel and swung up into the wagon. "I can see you're not about to change your mind." He looked down on her with a sad expression. "I hope you don't come to regret your decision."

She watched him drive from the yard. Had she thrown away her future? A deep ache filled her.

She watched until he was out of sight; then she fled to the shelter of the house, thankful to hear Granny's muffled snores.

Maybe Reverend Law was right. Maybe I don't belong here. But I don't belong anywhere else.

She looked about the kitchen taking in all the things she had learned to love. *Yes, love. This is my place as much as any. Maybe not forever, but until I have to leave, I might as well enjoy it.*

She began the evening meal and was rolling pie crust when Matt came into the room. He skidded to a stop and looked at her, astonishment blazing from his eyes. Lydia blinked before his stare.

"What. . .what are you doing here? I saw Law drive into the yard. Didn't he come to take you away?"

Lydia laughed at the bewilderment in Matt's face. "Yes, he came to get me, but I'm still here," she teased, enjoying his confusion.

"What happened?"

"I just decided I didn't want to go." Lydia turned back to her pie crust.

Matt crossed the floor in two strides and grabbing her arm spun her about to face him. "What do you mean, you decided you didn't want to go? Isn't that what you've always wanted? Some way to get out of here?" His voice had grown hard.

Lydia wiped her hands on a towel before facing him squarely.

"I guess I made it plain I wanted out; but when the chance came, I realized I wanted to stay. And so I told Reverend Law I wasn't going." No point in telling him the Reverend had been appalled at her decision.

Matt didn't say a word. Suddenly he grabbed her about the waist and swung her around the room. "Whoopee!" he yelled as he twirled her. "This is the best news I've heard in a long time!" He sobered and set her down. "I thought you would be gone when I came to the house."

The door flung open and Sam charged in. "I just saw Reverend Law driving down the road. Was he here?"

"He was here and gone already," Matt answered, grinning.

Sam stared at Lydia. "I thought. . .we thought. . ."

Matt and Lydia laughed together.

"You thought I was going to leave with him, didn't you?" Lydia asked.

"Well, yes, I did," Sam sputtered. "He said he would be back to take you away. What happened?"

"I decided I didn't want to go. I'm staying here." Lydia grew serious and looked from Matt to Sam. "That is, if you still want me."

Matt took his hat off and threw it in the air. "Yahoo!" he hollered. He looked at Lydia, a wide grin lifting the corners of his mustache. "Of course, we want you." He punched Sam's arm. "Boy oh boy, did we strike it rich today!" He hollered again and the three of them laughed.

Granny limped from her room. "What's all this racket about? You'd think a body could sleep in peace, but no."

"You can sleep any time." Matt grabbed her arm and guided her to her chair. "Fact is, you mostly do so it won't hurt you to listen to us once in a while."

Granny snorted. "Such carryings-on. It's not decent."

Matt clapped his hands. "Seems you don't think having any sort of fun is decent but it don't matter. Lydia's just agreed to stay on and that's news worth making a fuss about."

"Humph."

Lydia wondered if she'd seen the ghost of a smile as the old lady rocked back and forth, her attention on her knitting.

But smile from Granny or not, Lydia couldn't remember feeling so warm inside since before Mother got ill. It stung to think Arthur could so easily dismiss her, but at least there were two—probably three—people who appreciated her.

❧

The next Sunday Lydia prepared for church as usual. Although nothing more had been said, she hoped Matt would still take her. She stepped from her room and came face-to-face with Sam, resplendent in a navy suit and white shirt. His hair, the color of a ripe wheat field, was still damp. "I've decided to take you to church this morning."

Lydia swallowed hard, her thoughts colliding. She tried not to stare. "Where's Matt?"

Sam shook his head. "I'm not sure. He rode out a little while ago. Didn't say a word to me." He led her to the wagon, helped her to the seat, and climbed up beside her. "I don't know what he's got up his sleeve right now. Guess he'll tell us when he has a mind to."

Lydia settled back, her head buzzing with questions. Had Matt decided he couldn't be bothered to take her anymore? Or had Sam offered because of Matt's forgetfulness last week? She was pondering what this meant when Sam pointed to some cows grazing close to the road.

"See those cows, Lydia? They belong to the Schmidts. Notice how small and speckled the calves are? Now look over there." He directed her gaze to the hills above the lake. "See those pretty red, white-faced calves running about? Those are my cows with their Hereford calves."

She could almost see his chest swell.

"With the animals I imported from England, I'm going to have the finest herd in all of Alberta." He paused. "And the biggest ranch."

Lydia turned so she could see his face. "That's a pretty big goal."

"One I aim to reach." The muscles in his jaw rippled.

"I'm sure you will." She'd seen enough of him to know he would succeed if it depended on hard work and determination. Where had he learned such dedication to a task? Perhaps at home. "Are your parents farmers?"

"No," he shook his head, his voice growing hard as he stared across at the distant hills. "My grandfather—my father's father—used to own a good farm. It had been in the family since my great-great-great-grandfather's time."

"What happened to it?"

"My father decided he had more noble things to do than farm and advised my grandfather to sell it when I was just a boy." He spat the words out.

Lydia shrank from the vehemence in his voice. "What. . ." She hesitated, wondering briefly if it was a subject that should be avoided, then plowed on with her question. "What was it your father wanted to do instead of farm?"

"Preach!"

"Your father is a preacher?"

"No, not really." Sam sighed. "But he probably wishes he were. My uncle is, though. I think he calls himself an evangelist. They—and my mother—were involved in a revival about twenty years ago. That's when they decided they had a calling to preach. They left my grandfather on the farm alone. My uncle works in a mission in the slums of London, and my father took a job at the mill in town so he could be free to travel around and preach on Sundays. Eventually Grandfather's health gave out and he had to sell his land. He died six years ago."

Lydia stared at Sam. She would never have guessed his calm exterior hid all that resentment. She turned her gaze back to the road as she said, "And you came to Canada to build a new farm to honor your grandfather?"

"No!" he exploded. "I came to prove I can make it on my own. I can succeed and be happy without the religious fervor they think is necessary."

Lydia nodded. "So that's why it's so important you have the best ranch and the best cow herd."

"And I will have!"

They were turning the corner before Lydia spoke again. "What about their beliefs? Did you never share their faith in God?"

"I suppose I did at one time. I was taught that God loves us but sin separated us from Him and that Jesus died to take care of my sin so I could reestablish my relationship with God. I believed it and accepted it as applying to me personally. But," his voice grew hard, "I've decided to be a rancher—and a good one."

Lydia studied his face. "Isn't it possible," she asked, her voice low, "isn't it possible to do both?"

He turned and held her with his intense blue gaze. She tried to understand what his look meant. She couldn't decide if he was startled at her statement or thought her daft for thinking such a thing.

Then they were in Akasu and Sam turned away. Lydia sucked in a deep breath.

In front of the church, Sam helped her down then turned back to the wagon but instead of driving out of the yard, he tied the horses to the fence and strode across the yard to join her. At her questioning glance, he smiled and said, "I might as well go in out of the sun as wait around town." He gently took her elbow and turned her around, escorting her across the yard and into the church.

Lydia was relieved that Reverend Law was already on the platform. As he rose to announce the opening hymn, his eyes swept the congregation, lingering on her a moment, then widening as he saw Sam seated beside her. A smile twitched the corners of Lydia's mouth as she picked up the hymnbook.

After church, she paused and wiped her damp palms on her skirt and then there was no one between her and Reverend Law.

"It's always a pleasure to have you with us, Miss Baxter." He lowered his voice. "I hope you've had time to reconsider."

Lydia shook her head.

"Well, if you do, the position is still available."

She nodded and joined Sam outdoors.

People gathered around him.

"Sam, it's good to see you here."

"How are the calves doing?"

"Did you get that heavy rain?"

The men and women flocked around him, welcoming him and seeking his advice.

Lydia had never seen this side of Sam and was amazed at the way in which he was accepted, even admired. Rather than rushing off as she had imagined, they were among the last to leave. Norman and Alice had been gone several minutes when Sam finally turned to her.

"Shall we be going?" he asked.

Nodding, Lydia hurried toward the wagon.

Driving down the street, Sam asked, "Do you have something ready for dinner?"

"I have some cold meat for sandwiches. And there's still some rhubarb pie left." She hoped he wasn't wanting something more substantial as she hadn't prepared anything.

"Then I suggest we have our dinner here." With a decisive flick of his wrist he turned down the street to stop beside the hotel. He reached up and lifted Lydia down as easily as he would swing a child. It made her pulses break into a gallop despite her vow to treat the men like she would any other employer.

She hid her confusion under the pretext of smoothing her skirt.

Inside the dining room, the light was muted by the heavy

curtains and dark wood of the room. Sam touched her elbow lightly to guide her to a small table overlooking the veranda then pulled out a chair for her.

Lydia found herself very interested in the three horses tethered outside. Suddenly a menu was set before her.

"Well, now isn't this a surprise!"

Lydia jerked up and saw Lizzie. "Why, Lizzie, how are you? But I thought you worked at the store."

"I do. But I work here some of the time, too." She passed a menu to Sam who was watching them with open curiosity.

"Lizzie, this is Sam Hatten from the Twin Spurs Ranch."

Lydia turned to Sam. "This is Lizzie who works at Sterlings Department Store. She's the one who helped me buy my dress and shoes."

Sam rose quickly and held out his hand. "Pleased to meet you, Lizzie. You did a good job of helping Lydia select her dress. It's very becoming to her."

"Thank you, sir."

Lydia bowed her head to hide the warmth flooding up her cheeks.

As they waited for their orders, Sam pointed out people he knew and told her more about the town. Later, after the meal arrived, he asked if everything was to her liking. He called Lizzie over to refill her coffee. He was very attentive, but Lydia had difficulty concentrating on what he said.

"Have you always gone to church, Lydia?" They were bumping along on their way home—full of good food—the sun warm on their faces.

"Well, I spent the last two years working for a reverend so I went every Sunday." She smiled at the thought of deliberately missing church while in Reverend Williams's home.

"Before that I went when I was given the opportunity, and seeing it's considered proper etiquette to allow servants to attend Sunday services, I usually managed to go."

"What about before that? Before you started work. Did

your family go to church?"

So Lydia told him about her mother's death. "Mother spent a lot of time reading the Bible to me and talking to me. When I look back, I realize she was trying to prepare me. I think she knew she wouldn't be around to see me grow up and maybe she knew things would happen that wouldn't be pleasant. So she tried to tell me ahead of time how to deal with them."

They were silent for a while.

Finally, Sam spoke. "I'm trying to imagine how your mother must have felt. What sort of things did she say to you?"

"Maybe it was more her message than her words, but I do recall a few things she said, like, 'Give an honest day's work for an honest day's pay.' And she would read me verses such as, 'Seek ye first the kingdom of God and His righteousness and all these things will be added unto you.' " Lydia gazed at the fluffy clouds sailing overhead. "I remember one saying she had," Lydia's voice was tremulous. " 'Remember, no matter how cloudy the sky, the sun is still shining. It's the same with God's love. No matter how awful our circumstances. . .' " Lydia's voice broke. She took a deep breath and continued, her words barely a whisper, " 'He still loves us.' "

"I'm sorry," Sam touched her arm. "I didn't mean to stir up painful memories."

She shook her head and tried to smile. "Thanks, but it isn't that. I've just realized how little attention I've paid to her words, and I feel like I've let her down."

"How could you have let her down? I'm sure you've always done what's right."

"Maybe I've done what looked right on the outside. That was easy when I lived with a preacher and his family, but I haven't always believed the way I should."

"What do you mean?"

"Remember what I said Mother would tell me? That God's love is always there even when things seem troublesome, like a storm blotting out the sun? I'd forgotten she said that until right now, but. . .well, when things haven't gone as I think they should, I've doubted whether God loved me. I just realized how childish an attitude that is. It doesn't show any trust at all. I must believe God cares about me all the time if I believe He cares at all."

This time the silence lasted much longer. Then she sighed. "I remember something else she said a lot. 'It's not nearly as important what happens to us as how we react to what happens.' I guess my reactions have been wrong. Maybe it's time for me to grow up and stop looking for someone to be responsible for me. It's time I was the one responsible for me."

Sam nodded. "In a way it reminds me of my mother. Only I always thought she and Dad were preaching at me. I've never thought they might be trying to prepare me for some of the problems and decisions I would have to face." His voice deepened. "I felt I had to do things their way or it was wrong."

"And you found their way to be different than yours?"

"You might say that. I'm sure they thought I would follow in my uncle's footsteps and become a preacher, but I had no such desire. I've always thought they were disappointed in me when I decided to come to Canada and become a rancher."

"You keep saying you thought they thought this or that. Did they say anything about your choice?"

"Well," Sam shifted uneasily. "No, not really. They helped me pack and ship the things I wanted. In fact, they arranged to have my bull shipped over here. But I knew what they were thinking." He blurted out the last words.

"I wonder if you could have been wrong."

Sam rubbed his jaw. "I don't think so." He shifted on the seat like he was suddenly uncomfortable. "I don't know."

Lydia twisted her hands. "Now it's my turn to apologize. I'm sorry. It's really none of my business."

"No need to apologize. I thought I had everything figured out. Maybe I need to do some more thinking."

The house lay ahead of them. The sign to the right of the lane proclaimed Twin Spurs Ranch and bore the brand of the twin spurs.

Sam reined in at the sign. "I love this place. It's what I've dreamed of owning. I want to make it into a place known far and wide." He stared at the sign for a moment then flicked the reins to hurry the horses home. "I'm not prepared to give this up." His words were blunt. His voice final.

Lydia longed to be able to tell him God's love was worth everything else. But she wasn't sure she could. Not without dealing with her own foolishness first. Even though she had no words to offer him, she knew he was making a big mistake if he chose a piece of land—no matter how pretty—over God. It gave her goose bumps to think of him turning his back on God. Though she had often doubted God's love, she couldn't imagine planning Him right out of her life.

Sam would have to find a way of reconciliation with God if he were to be happy. She felt certain that success without God's blessing would be hollow.

eight

Matt, having declared a holiday to celebrate Lydia's decision to stay, sat in the back of the wagon on a box while Lydia and Sam perched on the seat. At first, Sam had hedged at the idea of taking a day off, then his glance lighting on Lydia, he shrugged and agreed it was time for some fun.

Pulling the box close, Matt leaned forward. "You're going to enjoy your visit to the lake."

Lydia caught her breath. He was so close, his face practically touching her shoulder.

"People come from all over in the summer. Everything from family outings to political conventions. You should have seen the one last year. All the fancy duds and all the bigwigs. And the food! It was. . ."

She didn't hear the rest of what he said. His breath against her cheek was like the playful teasing of a feather, only the thrill it brought was to a place deep within.

Sam chuckled at something Matt said and Lydia met his blue eyes, the expression in them as warm as the smile on his lips.

Lydia thought the men seemed different since the day she had refused to leave with Reverend Law. They were more attentive, more considerate. Sam brought a bundle of flowers almost every day and several times she'd caught him watching her as she moved about the kitchen.

She stared at the twin tracks disappearing under the horses. Maybe it was her imagination.

They pulled into the Youngs' farm and Lydia plunged her errant emotions into hiding, determined to keep Alice from guessing the confusion in her heart.

Norman helped Alice into the back and climbed up to sit beside Matt. The conversation turned to weather and crops and community events, leaving no time for Lydia to dwell on her circling thoughts of Matt and Sam.

It was ideal picnic weather with a bounty of warm sunshine and cool breezes. They had barely stopped the wagon beneath some trees when Sam, Matt, and Norman produced a ball, a bat, and gloves. Out on the sand they tossed the ball back and forth for a few minutes, then Sam batted the ball for Matt and Norman to catch.

Lydia sat on a blanket beside Alice swaddled in lazy contentment. She leaned back to enjoy the sunshine.

"Let's have a game of scrub ball," said Matt.

"Come on, ladies, you'll have to help us out," Norman called.

Alice jumped to her feet. "I think they're in for a surprise. I was always a good ball player at home. Could beat out all my brothers."

"Wait," Lydia begged as Alice jogged toward the men.

"What's the matter?" Alice asked over her shoulder.

"I don't know how to play ball. I've never, ever played it before. I can't do it." Lydia's voice raised in panic.

Alice rushed back to Lydia, grabbed her arm, and pulled her to her feet. "You'll learn. There's nothing to it."

The men gathered round.

"Sure, we'll show you what to do," Norman assured her.

Matt and Sam nodded in agreement.

The idea of being at the receiving end of a spinning ball made Lydia want to run in the opposite direction, but the others hurried to spots on the grassy sand. Sam pounded the ball into his glove, Norman hunched down with his glove raised in front of him. Alice moved out to the right then turned and hollered, "All right! Let's play ball!"

Matt tipped a bat toward Lydia.

"What do I do?" she asked, her voice a thin squeak.

"You take this bat and hit the ball when Sam throws it to you. And then you run like the fury to the base where Alice is standing."

Lydia took the bat like it was a bad smell and dragged it

across the sand. "Where do I stand?"

"Here, let me show you what to do." Matt turned her about, wrapping his arms around her, and lifted the bat in front of them. The pressure of his chest against her back and the warmth of his hands over hers sent a shivering shock through her body. A warm flush spread up her face. His sudden indrawn breath made her wonder if he, too, felt the shock of being so close.

The moment passed quickly as Sam called, "Are you ready?"

The ball whizzed toward them. Matt swung the bat, guiding Lydia through the motions. She felt the shudder and heard the crack as the ball arched through the air.

Matt grabbed the bat from her hands and pushed her toward Alice. "Run, run!" he shouted. "Go to that piece of wood!"

Lydia ran. At the marker, she tripped and tumbled in a heap on the warm sand.

"You're safe. Good run!" Matt called.

Lydia looked up and saw Sam and Alice both lying on the ground. Alice rose and dusted herself off. "I'd have gotten it, if you hadn't run into me," she said with disgust.

Sam got up, rubbing a spot on his arm. "What did you hit me with?"

Norman threw his glove on the ground. "Where's the ball?"

It started as a tickle in her stomach and burst forth like the ringing of bells. The others stared as her laughter rippled across the sand. They looked sheepishly at each other then they were all laughing.

Lydia couldn't seem to stop laughing all afternoon as they played ball on the warm sand, the gentle breeze cooling them. The others seemed to have caught the same tickle for they laughed as well.

"I've got to have a drink," Matt called at last, ending the ball game. The others joined him at the wagon for cool lemonade.

Resting on the grass, listening to the others laugh about the ball game, Lydia felt a wonderful sense of ease with them and she let contentment envelop her.

She turned on her side to stare at the lake, fascinated by the glisten of the water, sparkling like coins tossed into the sunshine. She grew aware of a deep calm. She couldn't remember ever feeling happier than she did at that moment.

She turned to study the others.

Matt and Sam lay with their hats covering their eyes. Alice was on her stomach next to Norman who chewed a blade of grass as he gazed at the leaves overhead. Suddenly Lydia knew why she felt so pleased with life. It was the first time she had friends her own age or felt she was part of a group.

Her gaze roamed the hills above the lake until she found the green-roofed house. How fortunate she was to have such a lovely home. A rush of warmth filled her as she studied it nestled in the hills. Of course it wasn't really her home; she only worked there.

She lay on her back and gazed at the leaves dancing against the sky. A leaf flitted down and landed beside her. *Drifting aimlessly like my life.* She jerked convulsively. *No. Not like my life. As long as I don't leave out God, my life has purpose. It has meaning. God, I will trust and follow You.* She allowed His love to flood her heart until she thought she would burst.

Even if it meant moving to another place. Even if it meant moving on and on for the rest of her life. For a moment she lay still, then a surge of renewal jolted through her and she jumped to her feet. Four pairs of eyes jerked open to follow her sudden movement. "I'm going to walk along the shore," she announced and marched toward the water's edge.

"Wait." Alice ran after her. "I'll come with you. This is the first time I've been to the lake. I want to explore, too."

Behind them they heard grunts and moans as the men struggled to their feet and followed.

On the lake several brown baby ducks swam in a V-path behind their parent. At their approach, the adult bird flew quacking into the air while the young ones darted into the reeds and hid.

"We should have brought swimming suits and gone in the water," Alice said.

"I wish we had. It would be fun to see the expression on your face," Matt teased.

"Why? What do you mean?" Alice turned around to face him.

"That's alkali water and it tastes terrible. I've seen men bring up their dinner when they got a taste of it."

"Can't you swim in it then?"

"Oh, yes. You just have to be very careful not to get any in your mouth. And you have to wash when you come out or your skin turns all white. I guess that's why people only swim here when it gets really hot."

Lydia's nose wrinkled as the breeze drifted across the water. "Phew. What's that dreadful smell?"

The three men laughed as if it were some special private joke.

"That's the water. Doesn't that make you feel like jumping in right now?"

Lydia shook her head in disgust. She couldn't imagine it getting hot enough to enter water that smelled so bad.

"Look!" called Alice, her voice high. "It's a boat!"

A cumbersome structure, looking more like a floating cabin than a boat, was tied to a post.

"It belongs to some people in town," Matt said.

"Would they mind if we looked?" asked Alice.

"I'm sure they wouldn't."

They found a narrow dock leading to the side of the boat and climbed aboard.

"Let's take it for a ride," said Matt as he helped Lydia over the side. She shut her heart to the pleasure springing to life at his warm touch and turned her attention to the boat.

The front part was a small room, more roof than walls, and inside a waterwheel had attached pedals.

Matt and Norman sat on small benches on either side of the wheel and began to pedal. The waterwheel turned and the boat eased forward.

Sam and the two women sat on the benches built along the back. Lydia lifted her face to the sunshine and listened to the rush of the water. The spray cooled her warm face. For a moment a sense of loneliness welled up inside her. She acknowledged it briefly before she dismissed it, resolving she would let nothing steal away her newfound peace and assurance.

She opened her eyes to meet Sam's steady blue gaze, gentle and kind as always. A slow smile crossed his face as she held his gaze. Shyly, she returned Sam's smile then turned to look across the lake. They were in the middle and no longer moving.

Matt and Norman joined them in the sunshine. Even nature was still as they sat contentedly soaking up the sun and the peace.

"I wish we'd brought our picnic out here," Alice sighed. "It's so pleasant I hate to go back."

"Today is a holiday. We can stay here as long as we like," Sam said, still watching Lydia.

"I think I could stay forever," Alice said.

"Well, I couldn't." Norman was emphatic. "My stomach is already beginning to tell me it's supper time."

"Oh you!" Alice moaned. "You have a stomach like a clock. It's never late for a meal."

Norman sighed in mock resignation. "I guess I can wait if I have to."

No one answered. For several drowsy minutes no one spoke.

"I'm sure the food must be getting overly warm by now." Norman spoke, his voice sad.

Finally, Sam roused himself. "Okay, Norman. I'll help you power this boat back to shore."

The others remained quiet, their eyes closed, as the boat

moved slowly toward shore—the lap of water spilling from the waterwheel soothingly hypnotic.

The sun was already kissing the treetops when they got back. Lydia and Alice put out the food while the men gathered up pieces of wood to start a fire. With an ease Lydia admired, Matt prepared a pot of coffee and set it over the fire to brew.

While they lingered over the food and washed it down with the almost-bitter coffee, the sky performed for them. To the music of the water lapping against the shore and the birds calling in the reeds, a medley of pinks and oranges danced across the sky and rippled over the lake. The dance slowed and the colors faded—almost disappearing, then sprang to frenzied life in the firelight. Lydia sat mesmerized as the flames twisted and danced. Glancing around, she saw the others also stared into the fire.

Matt rose to get himself another cup of coffee and throw some more wood on the fire. "I remember the first time I saw this country." He hunched down on a log. "I was driving fifty head of horses north from Montana, needing a place to winter them, when I saw a ridge of hills to the north of me. It had snowed the day before and then melted, except in the hollows on the hills. I thought it was one of the prettiest sights I ever saw." He took a long drink from his cup, wiping his mouth with the back of his hand before he continued. "I left my horses in someone's corrals and just started riding for these hills. When I got here I just kept riding higher and higher until I was right at the top where I could see both ways for miles."

Lydia knew it was the same spot he had taken her and cherished the memory even more knowing it was where he had begun.

"That's when I saw Old Man Burrdges for the first time. He was getting a load of firewood. He was a bear of a man. Not very tall but with shoulders like an ox and a big, bushy beard. Anyway, I got down and helped him. Could that man work! He kept a steady pace all morning then we rode down to the cabin. He asked me some questions and I asked him some.

"That's how I ended up running my horses in his pasture and helping him."

Matt fell silent, then sighed. "It's hard to believe that was almost four years ago, and now Burrdges is gone."

"I was sure sorry to see him go," Sam agreed. Turning to Norman and Alice, he explained, "Burrdges thought this country was getting too civilized for him so he went to live in the mountains. You know, he used to be a Northwest Mounted Police officer. Sure told some fascinating stories."

Norman was watching Sam. "Sam," he asked, "how did you come to be in this part of the country?"

Sam took a long drink of coffee before he answered. "I left England when I was seventeen. I had decided I wanted to join the adventure of 'opening up a new land,' as they said in the advertisements. I worked my way across Canada, doing whatever I could, saving my money and learning as I went. It took me three years to get to Alberta and another year of working farther north of here before I found this spot. As soon as I saw it, I knew it was what I wanted, so when Old Man Burrdges decided to sell, Matt and I bought him out."

"This is nice country for sure," agreed Norman, "but one of the prettiest sights is those white-faced red cows of yours. That was a smart decision, bringing Herefords from England. A real smart decision."

"I still think horses are better," Matt said. "At least they drive better and you can sell them anyplace."

"I don't intend to drive my cows anywhere 'cept to the rail yards in Akasu," said Sam.

Matt shifted restlessly. "Sometimes I understand how Burrdges felt. There are other places to see; new grass for the horses."

"Well, I intend to stay right here and build the biggest ranch in the area and raise the finest cows, too. And I'm willing to give whatever it takes to do that." Sam's voice held a brittle edge. He threw the rest of his coffee into the flames, raising a hiss.

A protest sprang to Lydia's lips, but before she could voice it, Norman rose.

"You can stay here if you wish," he laughed, "but I need to get some sleep and I prefer my bed to this hard ground."

"I guess we should be heading home," agreed Matt.

In a few minutes they were riding down the road with only the moon to light their way.

Later, pleasantly tired, Lydia reviewed the events of the day as she prepared for bed in the soft glow of the lamp. It had been fun to learn to play ball, but the memory of Matt's arms around her sent a shiver through her stomach. Shaking aside the memory, she pulled the chair out and picked up her Bible. Her thoughts wandered as she opened the pages at the marker. Life was good and pleasant right now, despite her confused feelings about Matt and Sam. But she must set those feelings aside and let God lead her where He would.

She turned her eyes to the open pages before her and read Isaiah 26:3: "Thou wilt keep him in perfect peace, whose mind is stayed on thee: because he trusteth in thee."

The ache that had been building behind her heart melted away to be replaced with a swell of gratitude. God knew and understood the longings of her heart. His way was best. She read the verse several times.

Her heart filled with peace, she climbed into bed to fall instantly asleep.

&

"It's a good thing we had that picnic when we did." Matt wiped sweat from his face and neck as he watched Lydia working in the summer kitchen. "It's been so hot since that we would have burned to a cinder on the sand."

Lydia sighed and pushed back strands of damp hair. Even with the summer kitchen, making bread and cooking meals left her gasping from the heat. "I hope this breaks soon."

Matt shrugged. "Never can tell."

"What are you planning today?" She hadn't meant to sound so sharp, but his comment about the weather made her cross.

You'd think he could come up with something a little more encouraging than "never can tell." She didn't think she could survive another day of crushing heat.

He shrugged. "Don't know. Seems too hot to do much of anything. Maybe I'll go lay in the shade."

"Think again."

At the sound of Sam's voice behind them, Matt spun on his heels. "Where did you come from? You trying to scare the liver out of me?" Matt growled.

Sam grinned. "Would you call that a chicken liver? How come you're so jumpy?" He chuckled as Matt's expression grew fierce.

"I'm not jumpy and I'm not chicken. Why are you sneaking around like a weasel headed for the henhouse?"

Sam laughed and playfully punched Matt's arm.

Lydia shook her head and turned back to the meat she was browning, knowing they could tease each other for hours. Usually she found it amusing, but this morning she wished they would take their noise elsewhere. Her head felt like it was going to explode. No wonder Granny had shuffled back to her room saying she would lie in bed and melt; the heat was so bad it made no difference whether she was inside or out.

"I told Norman we would come over and give him a hand with the last of his hay," Sam said as he ducked a swat from Matt.

Matt stared like Sam had suddenly lost his head. "In this heat? You must be loco."

Sam shrugged. "His hay is burning up on him. Of course, if you can't handle it I guess it's okay if you lay in the shade." He stepped back. "Maybe Lydia could even lend you a dress."

Matt exploded. "I'll dress you for that!" He lunged at Sam, but Sam was already racing across the yard.

He called over his shoulder. "We won't be back until dark."

A few minutes later she heard them ride out and heaved a sigh. The bread had to rise before she could bake it, but after that she would find something to do that got her away from the hot stove.

She tidied the summer kitchen, then as the bread baked, she returned to the house and quickly dusted. There seemed to be a never-ending supply of dirt drifting into the house as the heat sapped the moisture from the land. She couldn't imagine how dry everything would be if this kept up. And the bulk of summer was still ahead. Matt had assured her it was unseasonably warm.

"More like August weather," he'd said. Then he'd grinned and quipped, "There's one thing about prairie weather you can count on and that is that you can't count on it. It can change as quickly as a woman changes her mind."

She'd grinned and waved a towel at him at the time, but it didn't seem funny anymore. She looked to the sky. She'd liked to see one of those sudden changes right about now.

Somehow she got through the morning, but the afternoon loomed like an overheated furnace and she decided to take a blanket and sit in the scrap of shade provided by the scraggly trees on the hillside. Perhaps a whisper of breeze would drift over the slope to cool her. Or maybe she could imagine relief by looking at the lake.

Nauseated and exhausted, she drifted into an uneasy sleep.

Something broke through her troubled dreams and she sat up to lean her throbbing head against her knees. There was a difference in the air. The lake had turned inky black and churned like a madly boiling pot. Black clouds twisted like rags in a froth of white soapsuds. A chill wind raced up the hill and Lydia pulled the corners of the blanket around her. The wind increased, tearing at her scalp until the pins fell out and her hair whipped free.

Lightning streaked across the hills, thunder rolled like the beat of a thousand hooves. It was exhilarating and Lydia stood to throw back her head and let the wind tear through her hair. The bolts grew closer, momentarily blinding her as they zigzagged earthward. A crash shook the ground. A prickly sensation skittered up the back of her neck and she could smell gunpowder. She hugged the blanket around her shoulders. The sheer power and volume of the storm held her spellbound. So this was what Matt meant by a sudden change in the weather.

Suddenly an angry voice demanded, "Have you lost your mind, woman? Don't you see how close that lightning is?"

Stilling the alarm that skidded across her shoulders at Sam's unexpected intrusion, she turned to meet his flashing blue gaze. Before she could gather her thoughts, he grabbed her hand and almost jerked her off her feet. She clutched at the blanket but he yanked it from her and half dragged her toward the house. She scrambled to keep her feet under her. He didn't slow until he slammed the door shut behind them.

"What do you think you're doing?" Lydia yanked her hand away and glared at him.

"Maybe trying to save your skin. You make a lovely target sitting on the side of the hill. Don't you know anything?" Sam, breathing hard, stood with his legs apart and his hands on his hips.

"I was just watching the storm."

Sam shook his head and turned to hang up his hat. "Lightning isn't particular about where it strikes and it was getting pretty close to you."

Lydia didn't know which of her churning emotions was most predominant. Anger at his high-handedness or gladness at his concern.

She murmured, "Sam, I'm sorry. I didn't realize there was any danger. Thank you." He met and held her gaze. Lydia felt herself being drawn into a bigger, perhaps more dangerous storm.

"Well, I wouldn't want anything to happen to you." Sam's voice was gruff. "I. . ."

The door flew open and Matt strode in. "Here it comes. I made it just in time. Listen." He looked upward and pointed toward the ceiling.

Granny stumbled from her room. "There's nothing like a summer storm to shake things up." She settled in her rocker.

What had begun as a light patter quickly crescendoed into a deafening beat upon the roof. "Look." Matt snaked his arm out and pulled Lydia to the doorway where the three of them crowded to watch the rain falling in sheets.

"It looks yellow!" said Lydia, awed by the sheer abundance of water pouring down.

"Must be something to do with the light," Matt suggested.

"Have you ever seen so much rain? It's like someone is pouring barrels of water over the house."

A trickle started at the barn and ran down the pathway to disappear over the hillside. It increased to a steady stream more than three feet wide. They were about to turn indoors to wait out the storm when the yellow light faded, and as quickly as it had begun, the torrent slowed to a light sprinkle then ceased.

Lydia looked at Matt and Sam, wondering if they felt the same amazement she did. Matt's face wore a faint smile. Sam's eyes gleamed.

She stepped outside. A fresh, clean smell filled the air. The stream running through the yard had already died away, leaving nothing but a sandy, smooth trail. Lydia went to her favorite position on the slope overlooking the lake. The water radiated a silvery sheen repeated in glistening beads of moisture on every blade of grass. The whole world was highlighted in silver. The sun shone forth in blinding brilliance and painted a rainbow from the hills to the lake. Its colors were as bright as if one of the Williams children had used his paints to brush them there.

"I will never leave you nor forsake you." She spoke the words aloud, her heart swelling at the beauty around her and God's words of promise. A light touch on her shoulder made her jump.

"It's beautiful, isn't it?" Sam asked.

Lydia could only nod.

"Do you see why I care so much about this place?"

She wanted to say the right thing and sorted her thoughts carefully before she answered. "I can understand how you could love this place, but. . ." It wasn't his love for the ranch or this country that bothered her. She could understand that. But he seemed to think his love must exclude devotion and commitment to anything else.

"But what?" His question interrupted her thoughts.

How could she answer him when she had so often faced the same dilemma of trying to reconcile her wants with God's leading? Yet she was convinced that to pursue a course apart from God would lead to all sorts of disasters and somehow she had to try to make Sam see that.

"Sam," she began in a faltering voice. "I. . .I, well, I can understand your devotion to this ranch and this country. It's a beautiful place. I find myself drawn to it more all the time." She turned from the majestic view to face Sam. "It's just that you talk as if there is nothing else in life for you. You talk as if God can't be part of your goals. That makes me uncomfortable." She wrapped her arms around her to still the ache as she understood that not only was God left out of his life; he seemed to think caring about anything or anyone else would get in his way as well.

They stood looking at each other. His eyes darkened and she felt a power like lightning zinging through her veins.

A shuttered look fell over his eyes. He stuffed his hands in his pockets and turned toward the lake.

"This ranch is the most important thing in my life!" His voice was hard. He turned on his heel and strode across the yard to the barn.

Lydia watched him go. His words left her with a knot of inner turmoil and she ached with a sense of loss she couldn't explain. *I will trust God,* she reminded herself and gathered up her skirt as she crossed the damp grass, planning what she would make for supper.

Over the meal, she tried to catch Sam's eye. Afraid she had

offended him or hurt his feelings, she longed to make amends. The meal itself was a peace offering. She prepared all his favorites: fried steak, mashed potatoes, gravy, turnips, and bread pudding. But Sam steadfastly refused to meet her eyes, even when she passed him a generous-sized dish of pudding.

Matt pushed his chair back from the table. Oblivious to the strain between the other two, he sighed, "I feel better now. Not quite so hungry." He laughed at his own joke. "I was beginning to get a little gaunt before supper."

When the other two didn't respond, he continued undaunted and unaware. "We had to do some repairs in the corrals. The water washed right through one section and loosened some posts, but we got it fixed already."

He rocked back and forth on the chair legs contemplating the ceiling. "I think we better ride up to the pasture tomorrow and see if there's any damage up there." He addressed this to Sam then turned to Lydia.

"We'll have an early breakfast and take our lunch." He crashed his chair down on all four legs, rose, and stretched. "Let's get everything ready tonight." He snagged up his cowboy hat and hurried from the house.

Sam pushed his chair back.

Lydia looked up. His face was set in hard lines.

The silence echoed with things she longed to say and Lydia sighed. She must try to mend what she'd mangled. "Sam," she began, hesitated, then hurried on before she could change her mind. "I'm sorry. I didn't mean to upset you. I was only trying to help." She ducked her head and concentrated on her hands.

"It wasn't you," he said. "I made a choice when I came here. I chose to work at being a rancher—the best rancher in Alberta. Then you came along. You don't say much but the little things you say and do make me question my choice. Was it the right choice? Can I change my direction even if I want to?"

She jerked her head up but he looked past her as if his

thoughts were far away, then his eyes narrowed.

"Right now I don't want to." Again his face grew hard. "I still want to be the best. And I don't think I can do that if I let anything get in the road."

Lydia felt his withdrawal like a blow to her stomach, and aching to see him change his mind, she put her hand on his wrist as he twisted his coffee cup round and round. "Sam, there's nothing wrong with having dreams and goals. We all do. But what about people and what about your faith? Aren't they important, too? Can't you pursue your dream of being a big rancher and still retain your faith?"

Sam stopped twisting the coffee cup and stared at Lydia's hand upon his wrist. Slowly he raised his eyes to hers. Her cheeks burned and she jerked her hand back and hid it beneath the table. His gaze never faltered.

"What dreams do you have?"

His question skidded across her thoughts. "Why I. . .I. . . have dreams. Lots of dreams."

"Tell me what they are," he insisted.

She twisted her hands and looked about the room. She hardly ever looked at her dreams. Dare she take them out for public view?

"Tell me," he said again, his voice low and demanding.

Lydia glanced at him. Something in his eyes tugged at her. She lowered her eyes and in a barely audible voice, she began, "Ever since my mother died I've dreamed of having a home where I belong." Her voice grew stronger. "Not just some place where I work until I'm not needed anymore before going to another set of strangers."

"A home like this?"

Lydia avoided looking at him as she glanced around the room. It was familiar and comforting to her. She had cleaned it till it shone, mended the curtains, and filled the rooms with warm smells of spicy cookies and fresh bread. She turned her eyes toward the window. Beyond lay the hills and the lake, the flowers, and the immense sky. She felt her heart twist as she realized how much she cared for this house and this ranch. It would hurt tremendously to leave it. But more than that, she cared about Matt and Sam. They had become very special to her. It would hurt even more if she were never to see them again. They were like family now.

With a loud swallow, she got rid of the lump in her throat and answered Sam. "Yes." Her voice trembled, "A home just like this."

"What would you do to get such a home?"

"I. . .I. . .there's never been anything I could do." Pain swelled within her. "I have no family and I belong nowhere. I go when I'm told to go." She felt tears threatening at the back of her eyes and swallowed quickly.

"I'm sorry." Sam's quiet words threatened to undo the last of her self-control. "But perhaps you can understand how important this place is to me."

Lydia didn't answer. She realized how important it was to him. She understood his feelings but. . .is it possible for a place to be more important than anything else in life?

It felt like someone had jabbed her with a knife. She would not think about it anymore. As Mother always said—

The door banged open. Matt looked in surprise at Sam.

"I thought you'd be out to help get ready for tomorrow! What's the matter?"

Lydia jumped to her feet and began to gather the dishes. *What have I been thinking of? Dishes to wash, lunch to get ready for tomorrow, and many other chores. And here it is almost bedtime.*

Sam rose more leisurely, stretching his arms overhead and yawning widely. "I guess it is getting late. I'll just get my things ready then go to bed."

Matt shook his head as Sam gathered up his rope, his chaps, and a jacket.

nine

July first. Dominion Day. Canada's birthday and a good reason to celebrate, or so Sam and Matt had been telling Lydia for days, and she was prepared to believe them. Nor were they the only ones planning a day of celebration. For the past month the local paper had run full-page advertisements informing one and all of the upcoming party to be held in town. "Races. Ball Games. Live Entertainment. Fireworks. Picnic. Bring Your Own Baskets."

By the time July first rolled around, despite the lingering fatigue the heat had left behind, Lydia was bouncing with excitement. She'd been to fairs before, but this time she would not be in charge of children or tending a booth or serving tea. This time she was going to be free to enjoy every activity while being escorted by two handsome young gentlemen.

Even Granny had decided she would go to town with them. "I'll go visit my friend, Martha," she announced. "I hear her husband is doing poorly. Maybe I can cheer her up."

Lydia grinned as she recalled the conversation. She couldn't imagine Granny cheering anyone up. She shrugged. Granny probably hadn't always been sharp-tongued and critical. Lydia wished, as she often did, that she could share the joy and peace she had learned in letting go of her troubles and letting God be in control—and trusting Him to do what was best.

But today she would let nothing steal from her happiness, and dancing a jig across the kitchen floor, she hurried to pack the food she'd prepared yesterday—fried chicken, potato salad, a pot of baked beans, and a loaf laden with raisins and cinnamon. All night the food had cooled in the cellar. She packed it into a large box and tucked layers of newspaper around the food then covered everything with a blanket to keep it cool for the picnic tonight. The cutlery, plates, and cups were already in a box, but she turned back to the shelf for a final check. Satisfied she hadn't forgotten anything, she grabbed up her skirts and hurried to her bedroom to change.

She was going to wear her blue dress. It was the most becoming thing she owned. And today she wanted to look her best. After she changed, she twirled around the room until she skidded to a stop before the mirror. Grinning at her reflection she brushed her hair into the soft roll Lizzie had shown her and stood back to admire the effect.

Her black shoes beckoned from the closet. She looked at the brown ones she wore. They would be more comfortable and decidedly more practical. Practical? The very word decided her. Why must everything be practical? She would wear the black ones and endure the discomfort of wearing them all day.

"Lydia," Matt called, his voice vibrant with excitement. "Are you ready? Hurry. We don't want to miss anything."

"I'm coming." She hurried out, breathless and flushed.

"Good," he greeted her. "Let's be on our way."

"Don't forget our picnic." She pointed toward the box on the table.

"Good thing you reminded me. Sure would hate to think of this sitting on the table while we went hungry tonight."

Granny had insisted she would ride to town in her rocker and was already seated there, facing backward, her mouth tight.

Sam helped Lydia into the wagon while Matt shoved the box to the front. Matt's horse stood tied to the wagon.

"You really don't need to take your horse," Sam said. "You can ride in the wagon."

"I know that," Matt replied as he swung up into the saddle and waited to ride beside them.

As Sam clucked to the horses a wagon rumbled past on the

road. Dust from another wagon rose farther down the hill. At the last turn before Akasu, Sam pulled the horses to a halt and waited for a wagonload of waving, cheering party-goers.

They stopped long enough to unload Granny and her chair at a white house with a white picket fence.

Then they passed the elevators and headed for the fairgrounds. The last time Lydia saw the open area it was empty and overgrown with grass. Now it was crowded with wagons, tents, and throngs of people.

She gaped. "Where did all these people come from?"

"Everyone within driving distance is here," answered Sam.

"Be careful; you'll wind your neck like a spring," Matt teased.

Lydia giggled. She was craning from right to left at a pace that left her dizzy.

Matt pointed and waved. "It's Major Davey."

Lydia saw a man in a dark green uniform sitting stiffly in his saddle.

"Who is he?" Sam asked.

"Major Davey. He's in charge of the militia for this area."

Lydia's eyes found another man resplendent in red jacket. Yellow stripes edged down the side of his pants. Sam followed her gaze.

"Why, it's Sergeant Baker, the Mountie. Don't he look like something else, though?"

Sam pulled into a grassy spot and unhitched the horses then led them to the fenced area. Meanwhile, Matt tied his horse to the back of the wagon before taking the lunch box and placing it underneath the wagon where it would be in the shade for the better part of the day.

"I wish people who own dogs would leave them at home," he grumbled. "They'll be over here sniffing at the food, but at least they won't be able to get into it." He had tied a rope around the box and lid.

Throngs of people hurried past, and Lydia stretched on tiptoe to see where they were going.

"Shall we go see where everyone is headed?" Matt's voice close to her ear was teasing, full of laughter.

She jumped at his nearness and asked, "Where's Sam?"

"Here I am." Sam's voice came from directly behind her and she jumped again. Sam and Matt laughed loudly.

"You two are rotten," she muttered, but her grin took any venom from her words.

"May we escort you to the festivities?" asked Sam as he and Matt each gallantly offered her an arm.

"Why, thank you, kind sirs," she responded in exaggerated politeness as she took their arms. Marching abreast, they crossed the trampled grass, laughter trailing in their tracks.

The crowd gathered like a flock of hungry chickens around a newly painted white bandstand festooned in ribbons of red and white. Banners on the roof fluttered in the breeze whispering enticements to the people to come and see.

The squawk of the band as it warmed its instruments formed the backdrop for the voices raised in greeting, the shrieks and shrill laughter of the children.

The bandmaster tapped his stick sharply, a drumroll drew everyone's attention, and as the band played "O Canada" the crowd grew silent; men held their hats over their hearts and women hushed the little children.

Lydia felt the tears pooling in her eyes. Her chest was so tight she could hardly breathe. It felt so good to be part of this country and part of this celebration while accompanied by two men who meant a lot to her.

Following enthusiastic applause, a gray-haired man in a pinstriped suit and top hat stood at the podium.

"I'd like to welcome everyone to Akasu's Dominion Day Celebrations. We are proud to be part of this great country of Canada. As is fitting on such an auspicious occasion, we have planned a day of festivities. It is our hope that. . ."

"That's Mayor Wright," Sam whispered in her ear. "He

tends to be a bit of a windbag. Let's hope he'll cut his remarks short or we'll be standing in the sun for the rest of the day."

Lydia hid a giggle behind her hand but soon clapping and cheering announced the end of the speech and the beginning of a program. A young girl sang, a gray-haired man gave a funny recitation, a group of school children sang, and then a stately older gentleman stepped quietly to the front and began to play his fiddle. When he finished, the mayor signaled for a drumroll as he stepped again to the podium. "Ladies and gentlemen. Boys and girls. Thanks to the generosity of the good citizens of Akasu and my own personal efforts, we are pleased to present to you a magician of some renown. Right from the city of Ottawa, I give to you Mikal the Mighty."

A dark, mysterious man clad in tight pants with a full-sleeved white shirt ran onstage. A bright red cape billowed out behind him. He stopped abruptly, twirling his cape to reveal a women dressed in a similarly bright red dress. Lydia blushed to see how much of the woman's shoulders and upper body were revealed. She glanced out the corner of her eye. Sam was watching intently, seemingly unaware of the woman's indiscreet state of dress. She turned toward Matt. His eyes restlessly searched the crowd at the side of the bandstand.

Lydia soon forgot everything but the magician as he produced balls where there had been none, pulled feathers out of a little boy's ear, and made scarves disappear into thin air. Then he swallowed a burning sword.

"How did he do that?" Lydia turned to Matt, but Matt was not there.

She turned to Sam. "Where did Matt go?"

Sam peered around Lydia. "Humph. I wonder what he's up to."

Then he turned his attention back to the stage as Mayor Wright announced in his stentorian voice, "Ladies and gentlemen. Boys and girls. We are privileged to have in our presence Major Davey of the Militia. 'D' Squadron, of the Twenty-first

Alberta Hussars, under Major Davey, will now honor us with a parade. I direct your attention to the field directly behind you."

Lydia turned and her attention was riveted on the horses carrying stern-faced, stiff-backed men. Four abreast, they marched around the perimeter of the field, a thin screen of dust rising from each hoof. The musky smell of warm horse-flesh drifted over the crowd. Lydia stood on tiptoe, her hand resting on Sam's arm. The movements of the horses were precise and measured. She studied the faces of the men. Their expressions were so serious. Suddenly, she gasped. Matt sat on one of those horses. What was he doing riding with the militia? He raised his hat to her and waved a solemn salute.

Lydia fell back on her heels with a thud. Mouth half open, she turned to Sam. "Sam, did you. . .?" Her words died. She knew by the set of his face he had seen Matt and wasn't pleased.

"Well, I guess that explains where he has been disappearing to." He shrugged but his expression was guarded and he quickly looked away.

The column of horses and riders swung down the pathway between the wagons. As the last pairs exited, the men all raised their hats and waved them over their heads then suddenly galloped away. The crowd cheered and clapped.

Lydia grasped Sam's arm. "What does that mean?" she asked. "Matt riding with the militia?"

Again Sam shrugged. "I don't know if it means anything. As far as I know, they just meet to practice drills and do some target shooting."

"Then why are you angry?"

Sam turned and looked her straight in the eye. For a moment he didn't speak. "I don't exactly know." He sighed. "Maybe it's just that he kept it a secret and I'm wondering why he did."

"Don't let it spoil the rest of the day," begged Lydia, remembering the silence and anger she has previously witnessed between the two men.

Sam stared toward the now empty field. Lydia gently touched his shoulder. "Sam?"

He took her hand and turned to face her. The stubbornness melted from his features and he smiled gently at her. "You're right. Let's have a good time and not worry about it."

The blue of the summer sky reflected in his eyes until she grew quite dizzy. She started to pull away but Sam grabbed her hand.

"Come on, let's go see what else is going on."

There were races for the children and a baby contest. There was a horse race in which the contestants rode down Main Street, around a wagon half a mile out of town, and back to the fairgrounds, skidding to a halt in front of the milling crowd.

Sam and Lydia stopped in front of a booth.

"Throw the ball. Win a Kewpie doll for your lady," the man in black-and-white striped shirt called, offering a ball to Sam.

Sam pulled Lydia to a stop and studied the stack of milk bottles.

"Let's see how we do on this," said Matt from behind them.

Lydia spun on her heel. "Where did you come from?"

Matt grinned and dug into his pocket for a nickel, stepped up, and threw a ball that tumbled the bottles. The attendant presented him with a Kewpie doll.

"For you," he said, handing it to Lydia. He was so full of vitality as he stood watching her, his hands on his hips, his dimples flashing. Lydia thought he had never looked more handsome.

He turned to Sam. "Now it's your turn."

Lydia saw the flash of his eyes before Sam turned and picked up a ball. His throw caught only a corner of the pins and failed to knock them down. Muttering, he picked up a second ball and threw it with vengeance. The pins tumbled down and scattered across the ground. Sam grabbed his Kewpie doll and stood staring at it. Then he stepped to Lydia's side.

"Another doll for you," he said. "That makes two."

He strode away, Lydia hurrying to catch up, Matt strolling after them.

"Thank you," she murmured when she was close enough for Sam to hear. The sudden change in his attitude confused her.

Sam slowed so she could walk beside him and Matt fell in step.

"I'm getting hungry," Matt announced.

Lydia shook her head. Where had the day gone? It seemed like only a few minutes since they left home. In silent agreement, they turned their steps toward the wagon. Alice and Norman joined them as they passed the bandstand.

Dust rose with every step, clinging to her clothes, sticking to her skin. She was glad to see one of the men had thought to put a cream can of water in the wagon. They took turns washing and having a long drink, then Lydia spread the blanket out and passed the food around. They were licking the fried chicken from their fingers when a man passed by shouting, "Ball games to start in half an hour."

The men hurriedly reached for slices of the raisin loaf then helped Alice and Lydia tidy up.

"Come on, girls," Norman urged. "We don't want to miss the ball games. This is what we've been waiting for."

Matt slapped Norman playfully on the back. "Yup, this year you have to play on the married men's team. It's sad," he said as he pulled a long face, "to see a good man go downhill so fast."

Norman remained serene. "I wouldn't count my chickens before they hatch, if I were you," he warned.

"We'll soon see who's gone downhill," Alice added.

At the edge of the playing field, Lydia and Alice spread a blanket. Teams were already drawn up, the married men against the single. The married men were up to bat first. Sam stepped into place as the pitcher.

Lydia flinched as the ball sped past the batter. As a single woman, she knew she was expected to cheer for the singles team, but when Norman hit a grounder that had Matt and two other men chasing it with their gloves to the ground, she jumped up alongside Alice and yelled encouragement.

Then the single men were up to bat. Back and forth it went, accompanied by a chorus of cheers and jeers. The score was tied, five each, when the single men came to bat again.

The first batter struck out, then it was Sam's turn. He stepped to the plate confidently swinging the bat, insolently tapping it on the wooden plate.

"Do your best!" he called to Norman at the pitcher's mound.

"You won't even see it!" Norman called back.

"Try me."

"Play ball!" yelled the umpire.

Norman wound up and let the ball whistle across the plate.

Sam swung. The crack brought the crowd to their feet, some cheering for Sam as he ran for first; the others cheering for the fielder as he backed up, preparing to catch the ball. Then the fielder tripped in a gopher hole. The ball bounced across the ground where it was scooped up by another fielder and winged toward second, but Sam rounded second and headed for third before the ball arrived. The second baseman threw the ball to third. Sam skidded to a stop—trapped between bases.

The crowd roared. Sam faked toward second but as soon as the ball left the third baseman's hand, he dashed for third. He dived the last few yards, landing with his hands on the base.

The crowd was screaming, "Run, Sam, run!"

Sam picked himself up, saw the second baseman had dropped the ball, and raced for home. The ball spun through the air toward the catcher. It smacked into the catcher's mitt, but Sam slid into home plate under the catcher's legs before the tag could be made.

"Safe!" the umpire yelled and the crowd was on its feet screaming.

Lydia, her voice hoarse from yelling, grabbed Alice and they jumped up and down together. Sam raised his arms in a victory salute as he ran off the field toward the girls. Lydia ran out to greet him, throwing her arms around him in her excitement.

"You made it! You made it! It was so exciting!"

Sam draped a hot sweaty arm around her shoulders as they walked back to Alice. "Thank you, Lydia. For a few minutes, I wondered if I would." He sank down beside her on the blanket and wiped his face on his shirttail.

Then she realized what she'd done. Her ears burned and heat crept up her neck. She dropped her eyes, sure everyone was looking at her, shaking their heads, and whispering to the person next to them. What was she thinking? She had just run out and hugged him! And in public! She pressed her palms to her cheeks to cool the burning.

A young boy carrying a bucket of water and a dipper ran toward them and offered Sam a drink. Sam drank several dippers full then offered a full dipper to Lydia. She took it without looking up but as she tipped her head back, she met his eyes and saw a warm expression. She lowered the dipper and handed it back to the boy. Almost afraid to look at Sam again, she darted a glance from under her eyelashes and almost choked at the smile he gave her.

The crowd's cheering saved her from doing something stupid like falling into his arms and she turned to watch as Norman delivered three fast throws and struck out a man. Then Matt was up to bat.

Two times he let the ball streak by him and held his stance. On the third, he connected, sending the ball soaring into the air. He had reached first base when the ball thudded into the fielder's glove.

Amid calls of "Too bad" and cheers from the married segment, Matt walked back to retrieve his glove.

"Too bad," Lydia commiserated.

"There's always next time," he said, winking at her as he and Sam returned to the field.

The first man to bat for the married men's team struck out.

The crowd cheered Sam for his good pitching, but the next man drove the ball high into the sky. Matt and another fielder ran across the grass, looking skyward as they judged where it would descend. Neither saw the other as they raced for the ball. Lydia shuddered as they collided, the impact sending both men backward to the ground. The fielder rose, shaking his head and dusting off his pants, but Matt lay still.

Lydia strained forward, wanting to run out and see if he were injured, but she stood rooted to the spot, her hands clenched at her side, forgetting to breathe.

Sam was the first to arrive at Matt's side and knelt over him. He spoke to Matt and ran his hands over his head, his arms, and legs, but Lydia could not hear their words or guess what Sam discovered. Matt lifted his head.

Lydia let out a slow, shuddering breath and sank to her heels. Matt sat up, Sam's arm supporting his back. They stayed crouched, heads almost touching, then Sam stood and pulled Matt up. The deathly silence was broken by a rippled murmur, then the crowd clapped their approval. Lydia shuddered, watching Matt push Sam's hands away, lifting his hands to indicate he was all right.

Sam spoke to him again but Matt shook his head. Sam nodded and turned to walk slowly back to the pitcher's mound.

The game resumed but Lydia sank to the ground, her limbs rubbery. A drumming echoed inside her head. A spinning sensation whirled in the pit of her stomach. Gradually, her body returned to normal, but Lydia could not seem to regain her interest in the game. A great weariness filled her and she heaved a sigh when there was an announcement that the married men were victorious by two runs.

"Matt, are you okay?" Lydia asked as the group walked to the wagon.

"I'm fine."

But his words were sharp, his gait stiff.

Sam and Lydia exchanged glances.

Back at the wagon, the men washed off the dust and sweat. Lydia eyed the lump over Matt's left ear. A bruise darkened his forehead and edged toward his eye. She longed to apply a cold cloth, but his countenance forbade her making such an offer.

Sam met her eyes as he lowered himself to the ground and settled into a lazy sprawl. Lydia understood his unspoken message and sat with her back resting against a wheel. This way they could keep a guarded watch on Matt. Out of the corner of her eye, she saw that his color had paled and his face looked drawn. She ached to say something, but his fierce expression made her shiver and she held her tongue.

Sam shook his head. "Matt, I think we should go home now. We're all tired and dusty and ready to call it a day."

"That sounds like a good idea," Lydia added, a tremor of fear skittering through her at how much the bruise had swollen.

Norman and Alice had joined them and murmured their agreement.

"No." Matt's voice was firm. "Not until after the fireworks. Thanks for your concern but I'm fine."

Lydia glanced at the sky. Although it blushed a soft pink, it would be at least an hour before darkness fell.

The others sank back like wilting flowers, except for Matt who pulled himself to his feet.

"There's no point in sitting around here with long faces. Let's see what's going on." He began to walk away. The others jumped to their feet and followed.

They circled the grounds, stopping at the booths, visiting with the neighbors, buying lemonade from the Ladies Aid stand, but Lydia thought of how quiet they were compared to earlier in the day. They walked slower, talked more softly, and huddled together. Each in his or her own way was trying to protect Matt. It seemed they all sensed he wasn't feeling as he should. She would have gladly settled for going home for her head had begun to ache. But the determined set of Matt's jaw made her keep silent.

Dusk descended and they hurried back to the wagon and climbed aboard to wait for the fireworks. In spite of her fatigue and the throbbing in her head, Lydia cheered and clapped with the rest of the crowd at the display. Her enjoyment was dimmed further by the knowledge that Matt winced at every explosive sound.

They were the first to pull out of the fairgrounds.

They stopped to get Granny. She looked at Matt sprawled in the wagon box and sniffed. "I told you no good would come of frolicking all day."

"He got hurt playing ball," Lydia said in a low voice.

As Granny settled into her rocker, Lydia asked, "How was your day, Granny?"

"Fine, thank you." Then she added in a more pleasant voice. "I had a lovely visit with Martha. It was just hard seeing her Tom so sick."

Darkness wrapped about them as Sam turned the wagon homeward. Lydia wished it wasn't so rough. What if Matt was hurt worse than he would let on?

"You're awfully quiet." Sam's words broke into her thoughts.

She glanced at Matt, his hat over his face. His horse followed obediently behind the wagon. "Do you think he's all right?"

"I'm fine" came a lazy rumble from behind. "Just a bit of a headache, but, Lydia, I wanted you to see the fireworks before we left. Weren't they great?"

"They were wonderful," she agreed, but she wasn't thinking only of the fireworks. His voice sounded stronger and the tightness that had burrowed into her stomach when he fell finally eased. It had been thoughtful of him to insist on her seeing the fireworks. Both Matt and Sam had been especially attentive and kind today.

Life was just plain wonderful.

Too bad it couldn't always be like this. But she pushed away the thought, determined not to let anything spoil her pleasure.

ten

They headed toward home, a cold wind tearing at them. Lydia shivered. She hadn't thought to bring a shawl and Granny huddled under the only blanket. Icy splatters of rain stung her skin.

Sam wrapped his arm around her shoulders and pulled her close. "Let me keep you warm," he murmured.

Embarrassment burned through her veins but the wind was unmerciful, the rain like sharp arrows against her skin.

"Thanks." She shivered so hard she could barely form the word.

By the time they turned into the yard, ice water ran through her veins and her teeth chattered until her head echoed with the sound.

Sam lifted her from the wagon. "Hurry and get into something warm and dry." He scooped up Granny and carried her to her bedroom.

Matt hunched at the doorway. "I'm soaked and cold," he moaned.

"All I need is for all of you to get sick," Sam muttered.

"The l–lunch," Lydia stammered.

"I'll tend to it. Now go get changed so I can look after the horses."

She needed no more urging and hurried after Matt. She didn't even wait for him to light a lamp but crossed to her bedroom in the dark and stripped off her wet things, piling them in the middle of the floor. Her flannel nightie was tucked in the bottom drawer. She found it in the dark and shrugged into it. With shaking fingers she loosened her hair and blotted it with a towel.

She ached with cold. Her insides were numb. Weakness

flooded through her and she thought she was going to be sick to her stomach. Moaning, she crawled into bed and pulled the blankets up, praying for warmth to return. She piled the covers over her head but continued to shiver. Her throat scratched and her head drummed.

Finally, she drifted into a restless sleep, tortured with dreams of being chased by indistinct figures. She moaned and tossed as she tried to reach out to the figures. Her attempts were frustrated by a shadowy barrier. Voices called to her. She tried to answer but couldn't make a sound.

She felt something on her brow and forced her eyes open. A shadowy figure bent over her and she tried to move, but she was tangled in covers. Someone spoke her name and she realized she was only dreaming and sank back into her troubled sleep.

Again something cool brushed her brow. She tried to open her eyes but could only lift her lids enough to see through the curtain of her lashes. A lamp cast its warm glow over the bed to show Sam standing above her.

Sam. She struggled to understand why he was in her room and why there was a such a worried look on his face yet his eyes were so gentle. Calm settled over her mind and she slept.

Someone pulled a nightgown over her head and insisted on washing her face. Lydia moaned and clutched the covers to her.

"Well, well, so there is a little fight left."

"What are you doing here?" she asked Alice.

"I've been helping nurse you."

Lydia lay still, letting her mind analyze her body. Everything seemed to be whole, but extremely weak. She wondered if she had the strength to pull her nightgown over her knees. "I've been ill, haven't I?"

"That you have. I guess you caught a chill in that storm. And maybe you were a bit run-down and overtired."

Lydia nodded. "How long have I been sick?"

"Three days."

"Have you been here all that time?" She could remember bits and pieces. It seemed there had been someone sitting with her offering sips of water, murmuring comforting words. She knew she had clung to those words and found strength in that presence.

"I came over the morning they found you sick."

"You must be tired." Lydia sighed, thinking how weak and tired she felt.

"No, I'm all right. Sam took turns sitting with you."

Lydia turned to look Alice full in the face. "Sam sat with me?" Was that what she remembered? She searched her confused recollections and found glimpses of Sam holding a glass of water to her lips, wiping her brow, leaning over her murmuring words of comfort. She felt again the peace offered by the soothing rumble of his voice, and hugged the memory close. "I don't remember seeing Matt." She didn't realize she had spoken the words aloud until Alice answered.

"Matt said he wasn't any good in a sick room, but he took care of the cooking and the chores and hung around the house like an overanxious father."

Alice lay aside the washcloth. "You really had all of us worried for a while." She bent and brushed Lydia's cheek with her lips. "Now, I'll leave you to sleep."

Lydia closed her eyes. But she didn't sleep. Something inside would not settle. She longed to see Sam. To hear his voice.

The orange glow of the late evening sun filled the room when she again opened her eyes. She lay staring at the golden window then, feeling someone in the room, turned to see Sam in a chair beside her bed, his head bowed, her Bible on his lap. He turned a page and glanced up, his eyes locking with hers. Mesmerized by their warmth, she could not tear her gaze away. A gentle smile widened his mouth.

"Hi." His voice was low. "It's good to see you feeling better."

"Thank you." An emotion jolted through her. She turned

away and picked at the covers. "I understand you helped look after me. I want to thank you."

When he didn't reply she slowly raised her eyes again. He smiled, his blue eyes brilliant in the fading light. "Actually, it was quite interesting."

She looked at him with a measure of alarm. Had she been delirious and said foolish things? She glanced away in embarrassment. "What do you mean? What did I say?"

"Wellll. . . Nothing really." He emphasized the "really."

Lydia began to squirm. Sam's hand came out to rest over hers where it lay picking at the cover.

"I'm sorry. I was just teasing and that isn't fair when you're not feeling well."

She blinked. It was difficult to breathe and even more difficult to think. His hand was warm and comforting and did strange things to her emotions. She wanted to turn her palm over and twine their fingers together. This lurching of her insides at his touch, this ache to look at his face, this strange fluttering in her stomach frightened her.

"You didn't say anything, though you did moan a lot. I'm just glad you're going to be all right." He squeezed her hand then rose to his feet. "I'd better go and let you rest."

He slipped out, leaving her with a head full of confused thoughts.

The next morning, Lydia insisted on joining the others for breakfast. Alice pushed her into a chair and hurried to fill her cup with coffee. Lydia barely had time to lower the level before Alice jumped up and refilled it. Lydia stared after her friend. "You act like I'm going to collapse if I so much as lift a hand."

Alice ground to a halt. "I guess I am acting like an old hen."

"Alice. I didn't mean it like that. It's just that I feel a little awkward having you wait on me." Lydia drank slowly, watching Alice over the rim of her cup. "Besides, you must be exhausted."

"Of course I'm not. I'm as sturdy as a fence post and I'm used to hard work."

But as they lingered over coffee, Alice cleared her throat and looked from Matt to Sam. "I think you can manage now. As long as Lydia doesn't do too much she'll be fine." She pushed her chair back. "So, if that's all right with everyone, I would like to go home."

Matt sprang to his feet. "Of course. You must go home and look after that man of yours. I'll go hitch up your wagon."

Sam helped Alice gather her belongings. "You've been a godsend, Alice. We all thank you, but I want especially to thank you."

Alice patted his hand. "I know, Sam. I know." She gave Lydia a hug. "Now you take it easy. You hear?"

"I hear." Lydia grinned at her friend. "Thank you so much for helping."

Alice nodded; then amid a flurry of good-byes, and more thank-yous, she drove away.

Sam and Matt stood at the closed door while Lydia sat silently at the table.

"I'll clean up and make some sandwiches, if you. . . ," Sam began.

"Why don't I go and saddle. . . ," Matt said.

"I don't know what. . . ," said Lydia.

They laughed.

"You clean up here; I'll saddle the horses," said Matt.

"I'll help—" Lydia began.

Sam said, "You'll do nothing!"

Matt nodded, his look stern.

Lydia sighed loudly, sinking back into her chair, and watched Sam dip the dishes into the soapy water, then slice bread and meat and make sandwiches. He talked as he worked. "Lydia, we'll be out haying most of the day. There'll be nothing for you to do but rest. Go back to bed and don't worry about supper. Alice left food cooked. We'll get by on our own. We did before you came, remember?"

She sighed again, feeling guilty, yet at the same time relieved, for she was already tired, and looking forward to her bed.

Matt stepped inside, addressing Lydia. "You are not to do any work today. Not even run Granny's errands. She'll have to look after herself. You go back to bed and stay there. Do you hear?"

He waited, looking at her sternly, until she raised her head and nodded.

"I hear and I'm already looking forward to obeying."

He smiled, his dimples winking. "Good. See that you do. You're weak as a kitten. It wouldn't take much to have you sick again."

"I promise to be good," Lydia said demurely.

Matt nodded his head, jammed his hat on, and left.

Sam hesitated at the door, twisting his hat in his hands. "I hate to leave you alone, Lydia. What if you get sick again? Or need something?"

If he knew how much I want him to stay. But it wasn't possible. He had work to do and couldn't be at her side all the time. "I'll be all right," she assured him. "I plan to sleep the whole day away. You'll probably be back before I wake up again."

He still made no move to leave. "I wish. . ." He stopped then jammed his hat on his head. "I have to go. Take care."

She finished her coffee then returned to her bedroom. But despite her weariness, sleep did not come immediately. She didn't know how to explain the way her thoughts clung to Sam. Shadowy memories of him hovered just out of reach. She sat bolt upright remembering his cool lips kissing her brow.

Or was it part of a dream?

Sucking in a deep breath, she lay down, trying to relax. Everyone had been so good. It was wonderful to know people cared enough about her to worry when she was sick. And to sit by her throughout the night. In her mind she could still see

Sam sitting at her bedside, the light illuminating his face while his body blocked out everything else—even her concerns and worries. She felt protected. Safe.

With a little mew of serenity, she slipped into a dreamless, peaceful sleep.

Lydia sat at the table sipping her cup of tea when the men returned later that day. They stopped inside the door and stared at her.

"I thought you would be resting," growled Matt.

"If she sleeps any more she'll end up like me," Granny announced from her rocker.

Lydia giggled. Granny had surprised her by saying how glad she was to see her up and feeling better. Then she'd added: "It's about time."

Lydia grinned at Matt then she looked at Sam, drinking in his kind, gentle expression.

She gulped. "I slept almost all day and all I've done is make myself some tea while I wait for supper. I'm starved. Who's cooking?" She looked back and forth at the men, her gaze lingering a second longer on Sam. He hadn't spoken yet but smiled at her and her heart soared.

Matt looked to Sam. "Pamper a women a few days and what do you end up with? A tyrant! That's what. What do you think we should do with her?"

Sam rubbed his chin and appeared to give the question serious consideration. He stared long and hard at Lydia, his eyes sparkling with diamond flashes of blue. "Well, looking at the dark circles under her eyes and the deep hollows in her cheeks, I suggest we feed her." He punched Matt on the shoulder as he said, "It's your turn to cook."

Matt put his fists on his hips and glared at Sam in mock anger. "And I thought Lydia was getting demanding!" He quickly began pulling things out of the cupboards. "But I'll do the cooking tonight." His voice was resigned. "After all, Alice left everything ready." His voice filled with mirth. "You'll have to take your turn tomorrow."

Sam looked disgusted then burst into laughter and began setting the table. Matt continued to gloat as he finished setting out the dishes Alice had prepared.

"If you ask me, that young lady was awfully anxious to get back home. It was downright unneighborly of her to leave before Lydia is back on her feet." Granny stopped her rocking and looked at the others as if demanding a response.

Lydia sputtered. "But Granny, she has her own home to look after and I certainly don't need any more nursing."

"Well, I'd like to know: Who's going to make my tea?"

Matt's expression darkened but before he could say anything, Sam spoke in a low, lazy voice. "We aren't that busy. I suppose Matt could stay around the house and run errands for you." He bent close to Granny. "Do you have an apron he could borrow?"

Granny gaped. Matt growled. Lydia giggled.

"I was thinking a nice one," Sam continued, "with frills over the shoulders." He ran his hand up his chest and around his neck to show what he meant.

Matt planted his fists on his hips, glaring at Sam. "I'll not be wearing any apron." He turned toward Granny. "As for your tea—"

Granny shifted back in the rocker to face Matt squarely. "Never mind my tea, young man. I'm perfectly capable of getting it myself." She jerked her head for emphasis then resumed rocking. "Impertinent young man," she muttered under her breath.

Ignoring Matt's sullen stare, Sam slouched his shoulders. "Does this mean you won't be lending him a pretty little apron? I'm so disappointed."

Matt stomped to the cupboard for a bowl. "You'll pay for this. See if you don't. You'll have to watch your every move. Check under your saddle for burrs. Look in your boots before you pull them on." A lazy smile twitched Matt's mustache.

"Don't forget to look under your covers before you crawl into bed."

Lydia grinned. Matt was enjoying this every bit as much as Sam was.

The good-natured teasing continued throughout the meal and while the men cleaned up afterward. Lydia smiled and chuckled often.

That night she went to bed smiling, the laughter and teasing ringing in her ears as she fell asleep.

Next morning, she lay in bed and stretched lazily, contentedly listening to the sounds of the men preparing breakfast. She rose in time to have coffee with them, lingering over her own breakfast while they prepared their lunches. They left and Lydia returned to her room. A glow of well-being warmed her heart as she sat peacefully at her desk, cradling her Bible in her hands and studying the picture of Mother. Suddenly she understood her glow of contentment. She was feeling cared for in the same tender, gentle way Mother always cared for her. Again that ache in her heart called. Was she simply looking for security? She admitted she ached for a permanent home, a place where she belonged. She forced her attention back to her Bible. She'd been through this struggle before and had promised she'd trust God to take care of her needs. She tried to shepherd her thoughts back to the words on the page, but her mind was especially willful today. Over and over, like a wayward child, her thoughts turned to recollections of Sam leaning over her, his expression tender; sitting beside her reading her Bible. He seemed different.

She shook her head. *There I go again, dreaming up "happy ever after" endings for my life. Hoping someone would rescue me from my lonely existence and give me a pleasant, permanent home. It's time I grew up and stopped daydreaming.* She gave herself a mental shake, but even as she did so, another image of Sam flashed into her memory. *Enough,* she scolded. Until Sam allowed God to control his life, Lydia knew he was not the man for her.

God, You are my comfort and guide. Help me to trust in You and stop looking for mankind to provide my needs.

જી

She rested three more days before she grew so bored she couldn't stand it and made a batch of bread.

"What do you think you're doing?" Matt roared as he walked in the house and saw the fresh bread, but his eyes lingered hungrily on the warm loaves and she laughed.

"Don't go getting all worked up. It's time I started doing a few things."

"You sure?" Sam ran his gaze over her as if checking to see if she'd done any damage.

"Very sure." Tipping her head, she grinned at him. "I promise I won't do anything stupid."

And so they allowed her to begin work again.

Slowly, as July passed into August and then September, she regained her strength. The long evenings of summer were a special delight and as autumn approached, she discovered new pleasures in the season—the golden wheat in Norman's field, crisp grass underfoot, yellowing leaves rustling on the trees. The countryside was golden in color and she felt a golden glow of serenity. But as the grain ripened, the days grew busier. Sam and Matt joined the neighbors going from farm to farm to help with threshing.

While the men were away, Lydia dusted the logs in the front room, scrubbed walls in the kitchen, and washed the windows throughout the house, scolding the flies that buzzed about soiling her clean walls and windows.

Saturday evening the men returned for a late supper. Sam's face was set in grim lines. Matt studiously avoided looking at him.

Lydia wondered what had happened.

The men sat down and began to eat without speaking to each other. Finally Sam growled, "You shouldn't have left

Price's this afternoon." His voice was tight. "You left us short a man and cost us a lot of time."

"You got by without me." Matt's voice was cool.

"It wasn't right. Everyone was tired. They didn't like you leaving us shorthanded."

Matt bent over his plate without answering.

Sam glowered at him, hands clenched into fists on either side of his plate. "What was so all-fired important you had to leave in the middle of the afternoon?"

Matt placed his fork carefully beside his plate then leaned back in his chair. "I had an important meeting in town that couldn't be postponed." He stared at Sam for a moment then picked up his fork and resumed eating.

Nothing more was said and silence descended for the rest of the meal. The disagreement hung like a wet blanket over them throughout the evening.

Next morning Lydia woke wondering about church. Would either of the men be prepared to take her? After the strain of last night she was reluctant to leave her room and ask, but when she finally gathered up the courage to open her door, she found Sam dressed and ready to go. There was no sign of Matt and she refrained from asking where he was.

As they drove down the road, Lydia longed to speak from her heart, but how could she find the right words when she couldn't even identify what she felt? Was it gratitude? An ache for permanency? A desire for things that couldn't be? She was glad Sam filled the silence with stories about the threshing crew.

As they pulled to a halt in front of the church, she pushed her confusion into a corner of her heart.

ଈ

The days were busy as Sam and Matt turned their attention to the fall demands of their own ranch. Lydia welcomed the time alone to examine her thoughts. Something had changed since she'd been sick, but she could not put her finger on what it was. All she knew for sure was there was a void inside her crying to be filled. Over and over she turned to prayer, seeking God's strength in dealing with her troubled emotions.

She had just finished telling herself again she would forget all about it when she was startled to hear a horse racing into the yard. She hadn't expected either of the men back until supper time, but before she could cross to the window the door flew open and Sam raced in.

Her jaw dropped at the sight of him. Flecks of foam from a well-lathered horse clung to his pants. His eyes brushed over her then scanned the room. He kicked the door shut and dropped his gaze to her. "Are you all right?"

His look ignited her senses and she forced her answer past a dry mouth. "Of course."

"Where's Granny?"

"Sleeping."

He strode to the windows and pulled the blinds down. "Is Matt here?"

"I haven't seen him since he rode out this morning. Sam, what are you doing?"

He hurried to her side and grasped her arms, pulling her close. "I was afraid I'd be too late."

eleven

"Too late?" His hands were warm and possessive on her arm, turning her insides upside down. "Too late for what?" She couldn't keep the wobble from her voice.

But instead of answering, he pulled her to the front room. "This is better." He felt along the ledge about the door until he found a key and hurried to lock the back door.

A shiver skittered up her spine. "Sam? What are you doing?" His strange behavior was unnerving.

"Get Granny from her room."

Granny had heard the commotion and hovered in her doorway. "What's all the ruckus?"

But Sam didn't answer. He dragged Granny's rocking chair to the living room then rushed around the room pulling blinds and closing the bedroom doors. All the while the tension mounted in Lydia until she felt ready to explode.

Finally, he pulled two chairs close to Granny, pushed Lydia into one and perched on the other, every movement so tightly controlled she knew he was holding himself in with a harsh rein. Coiling and uncoiling one fist, he looked into her eyes, something dark and probing in his steady gaze.

Her alarm increased and she studied his face for some clue about his behavior.

He took a deep breath and said, "There's a crazy man loose. He was seen headed this way." He scrubbed a hand over his hair.

"A crazy man? Who?"

Sam shook his head. "Some fellow living behind the hotel. He lived in a little shack with his wife and son. He shot them!" His voice trembled.

"Oh!" She couldn't think of anything else to say as wave after wave of disbelief surged through her.

"Some people heard gunshots early this morning and ran to check. They saw this man running down the street waving a gun. He shot at Mr. Church, the postmaster, but missed. He ran into the post office and threatened to shoot anyone who came near.

"Someone ran to get Sergeant Baker—you remember the Mountie? He sneaked in the back door of the post office but the man must have heard him coming because he bolted out the front door, took the handiest horse, and rode out of town. In this direction." Sam sprang from his chair. "Did you hear that? Did you hear a horse?" He grabbed the rifle off the hooks and filled his hands with shells from the corner cupboard before he strode to the window to pull back a corner of the blind.

The sound of air escaping over her teeth rasped in the quiet room, and Lydia held her breath as Sam watched out the window.

Granny groaned. "I knew no good would come of living here."

Lydia wondered what living here had to do with a madman in town, but she only shook her head, still watching Sam.

He dropped the blind back into place and slowly turned. "It must be my horse. I didn't stop to unsaddle him."

"Sam, what happened to his family? Are they dead?" She had to know before the pounding in her side would stop.

He shook his head. "I think they'll be okay. Someone sent for the doctor. Things were kind of crazy in town with everyone running around yelling." He moved toward the door. "I'll have to slip out and put my horse in the barn."

Lydia leaped to her feet, clasping her hands at her throat. "Don't leave us. What if that crazy man comes here? He must be demented." She rushed to his side and clutched his arm. "Don't leave us here." Her voice ended on a squeak.

His arm snaked out and pulled her close. She leaned against him, her knees as weak as wet rags.

Granny folded her arms over her chest. "I don't aim to move. If some crazy fellow wants to bother me—well, let him try."

Lydia turned from Granny to Sam, torn between wanting to be with Sam and knowing she should stay with Granny.

Granny gave a little wave. "You go with Sam. You can watch his back. I'll be fine."

"Well, I guess it is best to take you with me." Sam's warm breath whispered through Lydia's hair. "We're going to run for it so you stay close, hear?"

She nodded against his chest but didn't move until he pulled her to his side, braced the rifle in the crook of his other arm, and opened the door. He dashed for the horse, scooped up the reins, and headed toward the barn without slowing his steps. Lydia skidded after him, clutching his sleeve.

They ducked into the darkened interior of the building and stopped. Lydia panted as she kicked her tangled skirts from her ankles. Her heart racing, she looked about at the dark shadows and gasped.

Sam sprang to her side. "What?"

"What if he's hiding in here?" She wanted to bury herself in Sam's arms but restrained herself, forcing herself to be content with wrapping her hands around his wrist.

They huddled together in silence. "I don't hear anything," he whispered, turning away to uncinch the saddle and throw it in the corner, then quickly pulled the bridle over the horse's ears. "Let's get out of here."

They crept to the open door and halted. Sam studied the open yard, his gaze probing each clump of trees. "Lydia, did I leave the door open?"

She stared at the house. The door gaped like the mouth of a snake. "I don't know. Maybe."

They pulled back into the shadows.

"We can't stay here," Sam hissed in her ear. "He could be hiding in the loft right now. Besides, we can't leave Granny."

She nodded.

"Come on." He grabbed her hand. "Let's go."

Her heart beat a rapid tattoo as they inched around the barn and halted at the corner.

Preparing to leave the shelter of the building, she filled her lungs and gripped Sam's hand, then her feet were tripping over the ground in a desperate race for the house.

He pulled her to the wall next to the open door. She leaned against the rough wood, too weak to hold herself up. He signaled for her to wait. She stifled a cry of protest as he tore his hand from her death grip and edged toward the open door, rifle poised as he ducked inside.

No longer able to see him, her insides froze. She closed her eyes and prayed.

"Everything's okay." His whisper close to her ear sent a spasm through her body and she jerked her eyes open. He beckoned her to go inside.

Almost falling into his arms, she dashed through the door and Sam quickly locked it.

"My heart's about ready to burst," she groaned.

Granny called, "Everything all right?"

Assuring her it was, they gathered in the living room. The rifle hanging from his hand, Sam paced back and forth. "Where's Matt? He should be back by now. It'll soon be dark." He spun on his heel. "Maybe I should go look for him."

Lydia jerked to her feet. "No." He didn't even know where Matt was, and if that lunatic had found Matt, well, Sam could easily become another target. Besides, that would leave her alone. Except for Granny. A spasm clenched the back of her neck and she moaned again. "No."

Sam seemed not to hear her. "He can probably take care of himself," he mumbled, pausing to lift a corner of the blind. "I'd best stay here."

She was as concerned as Sam about Matt's absence, but at his words she almost crumpled. If anything were to happen to Sam—

Her thoughts skidded to a halt and she gasped. *I love him.* Her eyes followed him hungrily as he paced. Despite the gloom filling the room and the fear holding them in its palm, her lips softened and a wave of tenderness touched her heart. Sam. Gentle, quiet, thoughtful Sam. Lydia realized how much she'd learned to depend on him. He was the staying sort of person.

"I suppose we should eat."

His words bolted through her thoughts. Lydia was sure she looked like someone caught with her hand in the cookie jar and she looked away. "I'll see to it," she murmured, her voice distorted like someone talking in a rain barrel. Her cheeks burned and she was grateful for the darkened room.

Food was the farthest thing from her mind, but she welcomed something to keep her hands busy. Perhaps it would distract her from the tangles in her mind. Her newfound admission of love for Sam seemed ironically at odds with her fear of a madman on the loose and her worry about Matt's absence. It was difficult to sort out such a differing array of emotions.

She stared at her hands moving without conscious thought on her part and took a shaky breath. Nothing could come of her love for Sam unless—until he gave up resisting God. It would remain a secret locked securely in the depths of her heart.

The floor in front of the stove creaked, the blind flapped against the window, the wind whispered across the shingles. Never before had she noticed how many noises the house made, but now each one jolted across her nerves.

"Sam," she murmured, "the food is ready." The sound of his name on her lips was so unexpectedly sweet that her throat tightened until she could hardly speak, and her hands shook as she set the plate of sandwiches before him.

He placed his hand over hers. "We'll be safe here."

She nodded, grateful for his comfort. "Granny?"

"I don't aim to move my bones again. Bring me tea and a sandwich after you've eaten."

Sam sat across from Lydia, the rifle between them on the table. Its presence drove thoughts of love from her mind. Fear rose to predominance.

"Sam," she whispered, "how will we know if he's been captured?"

"Sergeant Baker promised he would let us know when it was safe. Until then he warned us to stay indoors and out of sight. This man is extremely dangerous."

A shudder raced down her spine at his words. She tried not to think of Matt out there unaware of the danger, but her mind flooded with pictures of him being held at gunpoint—or worse—and hot tea threatened to splash from her cup. She set it down hard, waiting for the trembling to pass.

Darkness closed in around them but no one made any move to light the lamp. Sam yawned and pushed his chair back. "Why don't you try to get some sleep," he said. "I'll keep watch."

She jerked to her feet. "I couldn't," she murmured. She could hardly bear to have him move about the room without clinging to him. The idea of being alone in her bedroom brought a cold sweat to her whole body and she shivered. "I'll wait here. Granny, you lie on the couch."

Moaning, Granny did so, pulling a quilt around her shoulders. Lydia sank into the rocker, suddenly cold and weak.

Sam stopped pacing and sat on a hard chair, the rifle across his knees.

Her eyes felt gravelly as she kept them wide, promising herself to stay alert, straining for sounds in the dark.

"I pray Matt is safe," she whispered.

"Pray for us, too," Sam answered.

ঌ

Slivers of light fractured the dimness of the room. Lydia stared at them wondering why the blinds were pulled. She jerked wide-awake as she remembered why she was in the darkened front room. How long had she slept? Sam's head lolled back. The rifle lay at his feet.

Her veins turned to ice. What if that madman had found them sleeping? She edged to her feet, pushing aside the quilt. Her hands lingered on the warm cover. Sam must have placed it over her while she slept. She wished she'd been awake to enjoy his hands pulling it around her shoulders. She straightened. There was no time to think about such things. She crept to the doorway and darted a look around the kitchen but saw no threatening stranger. She turned back to Sam, watching him sleep, his face soft and relaxed, his hair mussed. She longed to brush his hair from his forehead. An ache tugged at her innards. She loved him so much she could stand there looking at him for hours.

But she jerked away. She dare not let her emotions get out of control, nor could she ignore the reason for the thread of fear tightening the muscles of her neck. Gently she touched his shoulder.

"Sam." She spoke his name quietly, hating to wake him.

He erupted from the chair as if shot from the rifle at his feet. "What is it? Are you all right?" He grabbed her shoulders and shook her.

"I'm fine," she answered. *Except for the way my heart is acting.*

He scooped up the rifle and stalked across the room, opening the bedroom doors to peer in, lifting the blinds and peeking out the windows. When he had toured the entire house and satisfied himself that no one hid in a corner, he returned to her side, running his hand over his hair to further muss it. The shadow of whiskers on his jaw gave him a rugged appearance, which Lydia found disturbingly appealing.

"I must have dozed off at sunrise."

She nodded. His bleary eyes revealed it had been a long night for him.

Granny snored softly on the couch.

"Any sign of Matt?" asked Sam.

"I'm afraid not." She refused to think about it. All she could do was pray again for his safety. "You look like you could use some coffee." She hurried to the kitchen and stirred the fire to life.

Sam moaned and stretched. "Sounds good."

She made hot porridge as well. He ate quickly then continued prowling the house, periodically lifting the blinds to check outside. Several times she caught him yawning and rubbing his eyes.

"Sam, you're so tired you can hardly see. Give me the rifle and I'll watch while you sleep."

Their eyes locked and she felt his inner struggle, then he smiled and relinquished the gun. "Thanks."

Moaning, Granny struggled to her feet. "You can lay here, lad. I'll be more comfortable in my chair."

Nodding his thanks, Sam lay on the couch, his legs bent to accommodate his length, and closed his eyes. In minutes his breathing deepened and Lydia knew he was asleep. Still she stood watching him, drinking in every detail of his features, letting her newly acknowledged love wash over her heart in thudding crashes. Then she forced herself to turn away.

"I'll make you tea," she mumbled to Granny. She did so quickly then padded across the floor to check out the windows as she had seen Sam do. Everything looked peaceful and ordinary and after a few minutes she settled into the armchair. Despite her resolve to keep her mind on other things, her gaze returned to Sam. What would it be like to wake every morning to the sight of him sleeping beside her? Heat sizzled through her veins. She loved him so much.

She strangled a cry. It was impossible to imagine life without him. She tried to pray but all she could think was *O God, I love him. I love him.* Her eyes were dry but great teardrops flooded her heart.

She ached so badly for love. Only now she knew it was Sam's love she wanted.

She longed for a permanent home where she belonged, but it was his home she wanted to share.

But he had said so plainly there was only one thing that mattered to him. The ranch. His words echoed like tolling bells. Love and marriage. God, church, friends. None of these would he allow to interfere with his pursuit of success.

She knew he was mistaken in his thinking. He would end up alone and disillusioned, but he would have to come to that conclusion on his own. If she or anyone else tried to reason with him she knew he would clench his jaw, his eyes would grow hard, and he would refuse to listen.

It was several minutes before Lydia realized Sam's eyes were open and gazing at her. She imagined she saw tenderness in his expression. Embarrassed to be caught staring, she jerked away.

"Did you have a good sleep?"

"Umm." He sat up and stretched. "I feel like a new man." He reached toward her. A dull roar filled her eardrums, but he took the rifle from her lap and her senses settled into a rapid beat.

Sam prowled the room, checking doors and windows, then perched on the arm of the couch.

"If Matt doesn't show up soon. . ." His voice trailed off and he pushed his hair back. "I don't know what we should do."

Lydia shivered. "I can't bear to think what might have happened to him."

Sam jerked his head up. "Listen," he warned. "Did you hear something?"

She held her breath and tilted her head to listen.

"There it is," Sam whispered hoarsely.

She heard it. She thought she would suffocate from the fear lodged in her throat. A scratching at the outer door sent shivers through her body. There it was again. Her eyes felt as large as saucers.

Sam jerked to his feet and padded silently toward the kitchen. Lydia leaped up and followed on his heels. He stood in the doorway, rifle poised. A scuffling sound grew louder, followed by a grunt.

A heavy weight descended upon her chest, making it impossible to breathe. The room tilted. Sam reached behind him and pulled her to his back. She leaned into his warmth, drawing strength from his nearness.

The doorknob rattled. Thuds shook the door. Sam lifted the rifle and aimed it directly at the door.

Lydia's legs turned to rubber. She was afraid her weight against his back would affect his aim, but she didn't have the strength to pull away.

A muffled voice called through the door.

Sam stiffened.

The voice outside rose. "What's the big idea? Open the door."

Lydia jerked. Sam half lowered the gun.

"It sounds like. . . ," she whispered.

"Matt, is that you?" Sam called.

"Open the door." Matt's voice was muffled yet unmistakable.

They rushed to the door. Sam unlocked it and threw it open. Matt crashed to their feet.

For a moment, shock rendered them motionless. They stared at Matt, his clothes torn, one eye swollen, dried blood caked on his pant leg. Then they bent and pulled him inside. Sam closed the door and relocked it.

Granny called, "What's going on out there?"

"It's Matt," Lydia replied. "He's hurt."

They turned Matt on his back. "Take it easy," he muttered.

Lydia gasped, her mind feeling separated from her body.

Matt's left leg was crusted with blood.

Sam pulled off the boot and ripped the pant leg to the waist. "Get me some scissors. And get water and clean rags. This cut needs attention."

She raced to obey him. A ragged gash on Matt's thigh oozed blood. She bent to sponge the wound.

"This looks dirty," she murmured.

"Use some disinfectant then we'll bandage it up."

She brought another clean cotton rag and poured disinfectant in the wound before she covered it.

"That hurts, you know," Matt growled.

"Let's get you into bed." Sam helped Matt to his feet. They hobbled to the bedroom. Lydia waited outside while Sam helped him into bed.

As she stepped into the room, Sam asked Matt, "Did you run into that crazy man?"

Matt opened his eyes and stared at them. "What the scratch are you talking about?"

Sam and Lydia took turns telling Matt what had happened. An amused look crossed Matt's face.

"So you thought I was some lunatic and you were prepared to shoot me? That's a fine welcome home."

Sam's expression grew fierce. "You had us some worried. What happened to you?"

He smiled weakly. "Nothing very heroic." He closed his eyes.

Sam and Lydia exchanged a look and quietly rose.

"No, don't go. Let me tell you what happened."

They waited.

"I rode up to check the cows in the north pasture. On my way back I came through the trees rather than go around by the trail." A sheepish look crossed his face and he grimaced at Sam. "I know. You've warned me about it, but I wanted to see if there were any berries.

"It was getting kinda dark and I never saw the hole. Neither did my mount. She fell in it and threw me. I tore my leg on a tree branch." He swallowed hard. "The mare broke her leg. I had to shoot her." His voice deepened with emotion and Sam clucked.

"I knew no one would find me so I crawled back to the trail and waited until morning. Took me this long to make it back."

Tears stung Lydia's eyes as she thought of him hobbling home with his injuries.

"Sure is good to be home safe and sound." His eyes flew open. "Or am I safe and sound? You greet me with a gun and tell me there's a lunatic on the prowl." He groaned. "Could be I was safer out on the prairie."

"You're safe enough," Sam said, patting his shoulder. "They've probably caught the fellow by now and just haven't been able to get word to us."

Matt nodded. His eyes closed. Lydia and Sam watched until they saw the steady rise and fall of his chest and knew he was asleep.

Granny gave them a sharp look as they slipped out of the bedroom. "I suppose he was up to some foolishness."

"His horse fell in a hole," Sam answered, a hint of annoyance in his voice.

Granny blinked once then studied her knitting.

There seemed to be little to do but wait. Lydia went to the kitchen and made coffee, breathing a silent prayer of thanks for Matt's safe return.

She and Sam lingered over coffee. Lydia turned the cup round and round, starting as Sam set his cup down. The waiting was making her jumpy. She thought she could hear hooves drumming across the yard.

Sam jerked to his feet, grabbing the rifle and heading for the door.

A voice called out, "Hello, Twin Spurs! Anybody home? It's Sergeant Baker."

Sam threw the door open. "Come on in, Baker. Sure hope

you've got good news."

The Mountie strolled into the kitchen, removing his broad-brimmed hat. Lydia felt a twinge of sympathy at his red-rimmed eyes and the dark smudges under them. He sank into the chair Sam pulled out for him.

"We got the man two hours ago," he said. "He's on a train to Calgary with two armed guards. His wife and son have only flesh wounds, but they'll be safe now." He looked around the room, alert to every detail. "I don't see Matt."

"He's here but I tell you. . ." Sam launched into a tale of Matt's adventures.

"I'd better take a look at him in case he needs a doctor." The Mountie rose to his feet. "I could send one out from Akasu if he does."

Matt woke as they entered the room. One eye was swollen and surrounded by purple bruises.

As he examined the injuries, Sergeant Baker kept up a stream of small talk. Lydia understood it was his way of distracting Matt as he probed the leg wound.

"Haven't you anything better to do than poke at a fellow when he's down," Matt grumbled, glaring at the man.

"Everything looks like it will mend." Baker straightened. "But I see his temper hasn't improved."

"Aren't you supposed to be looking for a madman or something?"

The Mountie smiled. "I've been working while you slept. He's in custody."

Matt glowered but with one eye swollen half shut it lacked fierceness.

Lydia grinned.

Sam choked back a chuckle.

twelve

"What do you think you're doing?" Sam's angry voice rang from the bedroom.

Her hands poised above the pancakes she was frying, Lydia stopped to listen. Matt's rumble carried to her but she couldn't make out his words.

"You're staying right there." Sam stomped from the room. "Take him some breakfast and make sure he stays in bed."

Lydia finished the breakfast tray and hurried to the bedroom. She set the tray on a stool. "Here's your breakfast."

"Take it back to the kitchen. I'm getting up." Matt glared at her.

She sat on the edge of the bed and crossed her arms. "I'm staying right here. Eat."

Their eyes locked.

"Pass the food." The expression on his face remained cross.

"That's better." She moved the tray closer. "I'm to keep you in bed today."

"How do you propose to do that?"

She shrugged. "Any way I can." Her voice softened. "I'm not about to let you take any chances. Do you have any idea how worried we were?"

He looked at her crossly. "At least you were with Sam. Seems that's the way it should be."

"Whatever do you mean?" She stared at him.

"Oh, come on. I've seen the way you look at him. You can't keep your eyes off him." He lifted his fork, eyeing her grumpily.

"Oh, Matt. I—" She fled the room, and his knowing look. Her feelings had been riding high since she'd acknowledged to herself how much she loved Sam—a love that swelled and grew as she rejoiced over it. At times she could barely keep from dancing across the floor.

Now her joyous emotions collapsed. She had to keep her love hidden. How long, she wondered, could she keep it a secret? Forever, she vowed. Sam must never guess. She pressed her hand to her chest.

Somehow she had to get Matt to agree to keep her secret. She retraced her steps to the bedroom.

"I'm done. You can take the tray," he mumbled.

"Matt," she began, forcing the words past the tightness in her throat. "Promise you won't say anything to Sam."

"You should both come to your senses," he said crossly.

"I don't know what you mean."

"I know you don't." He waved her away. "But don't worry." He closed his eyes.

He hadn't given his promise and she hesitated, wanting him to say so much more, but she knew he had said all he intended, and with her insides feeling like shattered glass she left the room.

The day passed in a fog of worry. If Matt had read her face, Sam could do the same. She'd have to be a lot more careful, learning to disguise the way her heart lurched when he came in the room, the way her eyes sought him when he was near, the ache she felt when he left. If she didn't—if he guessed how she felt—her mouth dried so suddenly she almost choked.

The next morning Matt limped out to the table despite the heated words Lydia heard from the bedroom.

"Man can't eat lying on his back," he grumbled. "Besides, it's only a little scratch."

Sam glowered at him, but Matt stayed seated until Sam left the house, then he rose and grabbed his hat.

"Matt, shouldn't you be taking it easy?"

"Got things I gotta do," he mumbled, and left the house. A few minutes later she heard a horse ride from the yard.

She stared around the room, her thoughts jerking from

Matt's foolishness at not resting his leg, to Sam—she closed her eyes. She wouldn't let her thoughts dwell on him and what she wanted but couldn't have. Perhaps work would take her mind off her worries. She got out her cleaning supplies and attacked the stove. But all too soon she forgot the brush in her hand as she mentally listed things about Sam she found appealing—his strong jaw, his heavenly blue eyes, his slim build, his quiet strength, his deep sense of devotion. She sighed. That deep sense of devotion would mean her love would go unrequited. Sam had made it plain nothing would take the place of the ranch in his heart and mind. There was no room for God and certainly no room for a little servant girl with nothing to offer.

Picking up her forgotten brush, she returned to her task determined more than ever that she would never let her guard down.

She scoured the stove until it shone.

With the same frenzy, she scrubbed the floors.

She was peeling potatoes when the door opened.

Matt entered carrying a squirming black pup.

She sprang to her feet. "What a cute little fellow!" The pup wriggled wildly, licking her fingers and trying to reach her face to lick it. She laughed. "Who owns him?"

Matt placed the puppy in her arms. "He's yours."

She stared at him and then at Sam who entered behind him. Sam shook his head. "I don't understand. You always said you wouldn't have a dog on the place."

"I never had much use for a dog," Matt admitted. "But I thought it was a good idea for Lydia to have a watchdog." He paused and stepped aside so he could see them both. "Especially now."

"Now?" she asked, lifting her head from rubbing against the puppy fur.

He nodded. "Sit down. Both of you. I have something to tell you."

Lydia took a chair, more curious than anything. What could Matt have to say that made him twist his hat so badly?

"Remember when you were mad because I left the threshing crew?" He addressed Sam who nodded without speaking.

"I said there was something I had to take care of."

Again Sam nodded.

Matt took a deep breath. "I signed up to join the army."

Sam half stood. His mouth opened and closed and then he dropped back to the chair.

Matt hurried on. "I'll be leaving as soon as I can make arrangements. I'm off to Ottawa for my training."

The silence greeting his words went on and on.

"What about the ranch?" Sam pushed his hair back from his forehead.

"I'll leave you in complete control." Matt spoke softly. "You can run it as you see fit."

Sam shook his head, "I don't understand. How can you just walk away from everything?"

"I'm not walking away," Matt protested. "I'm doing my duty as I see it." He gulped and hurried on. "I think we're about to see problems in Europe."

"It's halfway around the world." Sam almost shouted.

"Yes, and your family may well be in danger."

At Matt's words, Sam subsided.

When Matt spoke again, his voice was low, tight with emotion. "I thought you'd understand." He rose and stared at Lydia. "That's why I got Lydia the pup."

She lifted her face to him but his features were blurred behind a veil of tears. Everything was changing so fast she couldn't breathe. She choked back the tears pooling in her throat. She wanted to grab hold of time and force it to stand still. She blinked hard. She didn't want Matt to leave. She feared for his safety.

And it meant she'd be losing Sam as well. She couldn't stay now. She'd have to find another place. A moan tore at her throat. She failed to stifle it completely.

Matt watched her through narrowed eyes and she lowered her gaze to hide her pain.

"Sam," Matt began, his voice hard, "if you're half the man I think you are, you'll marry Lydia and give her the protection of your name."

A roaring sound filled Lydia's eardrums. She couldn't breathe. She couldn't move. "That's not necessary," she muttered.

"You're both daft," Matt muttered. "Your love for each other is as plain as the pink tongue that pup is scrubbing Lydia's face with." He jammed his hat on his head. "You've hid it from no one but yourselves." He marched to the door. "I'm riding to the top of the hill."

The door closed behind him. Unable to face Sam, Lydia buried her face against the squirming puppy.

Suddenly Sam squatted in front of her and tipped her chin up with his finger. "Is it true?"

Avoiding his gaze, she asked, "Is what true?"

He clasped her chin more firmly, forcing her to look into his eyes. She held her breath at what she saw. "I love you, Lydia. Do you love me?"

His blue eyes pierced through her defenses and melted her embarrassment as quickly as snow before a fire. She nodded.

He leaned toward her and covered her lips with his. A shock raced through her veins freeing the love she had tried to hide.

But she couldn't let it have free rein.

"I don't understand," she murmured, turning her face away from the temptation of his lips. "You said there was room for nothing but the ranch."

He laughed, the sound rippling through her veins until she was sure she quivered all over.

"I did say something like that, didn't I?"

She tipped her head back to look in his eyes. At his warm

look her heart somersaulted and danced, but she forced herself to forge ahead with her question. "You did. What happened?"

"I guess it started when you were sick." He kissed her cheeks then sighing deeply, pulled away. "I was so worried about you. I knew then that I love you. I wanted to pray for you to get well, but I knew I didn't have the right after I said I didn't want God anymore. I thought being a rancher was more important than knowing Him." He kissed her on the temple and pulled her toward him.

Reluctantly, she pulled away. "You were saying?" The words practically strangled in her throat.

He laughed low and she knew she hadn't fooled him. "I wanted to change but it was hard. For years I lived thinking all that mattered was being the best rancher. And all of a sudden I knew it wasn't enough, yet it wasn't easy to change. I guess I finally gave in the other night as you slept in Granny's chair and I kept guard. As I watched you sleeping, I realized the ranch would mean nothing without you and that God was calling me back to Him through you. That's when I quit fighting God and said I wanted Him back in my life. I meant it."

He jerked a chair out with his foot and sat down, pulling her to his lap. His arms tightened around her. "And life has been a lot more beautiful since I gave up trying to have my way."

She could no longer contain her love. It burst free like a thousand blossoms touched by the sun opening to release their perfume. The puppy slipped from her lap and she leaned into Sam's embrace, wrapping her arms around his neck, letting her fingers explore the silkiness of his hair. He tasted like every sweet thing she had ever tasted. Hungrily she returned his kiss, telling him in the only way possible how much she loved him and ached for his love. She snuggled against him, reveling in the warmth of his arms.

When he pushed her away, she mumbled in protest.

He laughed and shook her gently. "I want to see your face

when I say this." He lifted her chin with his finger. Their gazes locked. "Lydia, I love you. Will you marry me?"

She nodded, unable to speak. Tears flowed down her cheeks.

"Don't cry," he begged.

"I'm not," she laughed, the tears continuing to flow.

Someday, when she could talk without laughing and crying at the same time, she would explain her joy. God had answered her prayer for a home of her own in a way far beyond her expectations.

Not only had He given her a home, He had sent her Sam.

Silently, she thanked God for the gift His perfect love had supplied. Then her thoughts were swept away as Sam's lips captured hers.

epilogue

It was the brightest day in October, and Lydia couldn't stop smiling as she clung to Sam's hand and buried her face in the bouquet of wildflowers he'd picked.

He'd shaken his head over it. "Not much left this time of year."

She'd laughed. "Heads of wheat and a bundle of cattails would make me happy." Flowers were nice, but now that she was secure in the knowledge of Sam's love, she needed nothing more to make her happy.

The skirt of her white lawn dress caught in the breeze, tickling her legs.

Everything had happened so quickly.

Matt had agreed to wait a few days before leaving for Ottawa. "As long as it's by the end of next week."

Lizzie had found the perfect dress for her.

Reverend Law had agreed to do the honors.

And so this very morning she and Sam had been joined in holy matrimony.

There'd been only a handful of people at the wedding. Matt, of course, Alice and Norman, Lizzie, and Granny.

Now Granny was with her friend, Martha. Despite Granny's sharp tongue, Lydia knew she would miss the older lady.

"I wish you all the best," Granny had said when Lydia told her she and Sam were to be married in a few days. "You deserve it." She'd rocked hard for a moment then added, "It works out for me, too. Martha's been after me to come and live with her ever since Tom died, but I said I couldn't leave you alone with those two scallywags."

Lydia hugged Granny. "Thank you for being here."

"Go away with you, child."

Lydia was sure she saw the glisten of tears in the faded eyes. "I'm glad for you." She squeezed Granny's hand. "Just don't shut out God's love."

Granny stared straight ahead, as usual ignoring Lydia's attempts to tell her about God. But suddenly, Granny faced Lydia squarely.

"I've always been a believer, but I guess I let bitterness creep in until it pushed everything else away." She nodded, her eyes shining. "You made me see it didn't have to be that way."

The wail of the train whistle echoed down the tracks and the engine huffed and puffed to a halt.

Matt stood before them. "I guess this is it."

Sam handed him a parcel. "This is from Lydia and me."

Matt raised his eyebrows. "What is it?"

"Open it and see."

He tore the paper off. "A Bible?" He turned it over several times. "Thank you." His voice was strained. "I've been thinking I might need more than my wits and good looks," he winked at Lydia, "to keep me alive."

She threw her arms around him. "Matt, I'm going to miss you so much. We'll pray for you every day. You take care, hear?"

He hugged her tight. "You, too, Mrs. Hatten. Mrs. Hatten—sounds good, doesn't it?"

She nodded, holding him a moment more before he freed her.

He turned to Sam and gripped his hand. "You take care of things now."

"I will. You take care of yourself."

A lump grew in Lydia's throat as the men gripped each other with both hands.

"All aboard!"

The handclasp ended. Matt picked up his gear. "I guess this is it." With a crooked smile for Lydia and a sober-faced nod for Sam, he climbed into the train, pausing for a final wave.

The train snorted, belched smoke and jerked away.

Matt was gone.

Sam grabbed her hand as they watched the train fade out of sight, then he pulled her around to face him.

"Well, Lydia Hatten, let's go home."

At the look of love and pride in his face, Lydia's sadness fled. Together they would face the future and build a home filled with love and laughter.

A Letter To Our Readers

Dear Reader:

In order that we might better contribute to your reading enjoyment, we would appreciate your taking a few minutes to respond to the following questions. We welcome your comments and read each form and letter we receive. When completed, please return to the following:

Rebecca Germany, Fiction Editor
Heartsong Presents
PO Box 719
Uhrichsville, Ohio 44683

1. Did you enjoy reading *The Heart Seeks a Home?*
   ❑ Very much. I would like to see more books
      by this author!
   ❑ Moderately
      I would have enjoyed it more if _____
      _____
      _____

2. Are you a member of **Heartsong Presents**? Yes ❑ No ❑
   If no, where did you purchase this book? _____
   _____

3. How would you rate, on a scale from 1 (poor) to 5 (superior),
   the cover design? _____

4. On a scale from 1 (poor) to 10 (superior), please rate the
   following elements.

   _____ Heroine   _____ Plot

   _____ Hero   _____ Inspirational theme

   _____ Setting   _____ Secondary characters

5. These characters were special because_____
   _____
   _____

6. How has this book inspired your life?_____
   _____
   _____

7. What settings would you like to see covered in future
   Heartsong Presents books?_____
   _____
   _____

8. What are some inspirational themes you would like to see
   treated in future books?_____
   _____
   _____

9. Would you be interested in reading other **Heartsong
   Presents** titles?   Yes ❑   No ❑

10. Please check your age range:
    ❑ Under 18   ❑ 18-24   ❑ 25-34
    ❑ 35-45   ❑ 46-55   ❑ Over 55

11. How many hours per week do you read?_____

Name _____

Occupation _____

Address _____

City _____ State _____ Zip _____

Experience a family

saga that begins in 1860 when the painting of a homestead is first given to a young bride who leaves her beloved home of Laurelwood. Then follow the painting through a legacy of love that touches down in the years 1890, 1969, and finally today. Authors Sally Laity, Andrea Boeshaar, Yvonne Lehman, and DiAnn Mills have worked together to create a timeless treasure of four novellas in one collection.

paperback, 352 pages, 5 ⁹⁄₁₆" x 8"

····Hearts♥ng····

HEARTSONG PRESENTS TITLES AVAILABLE NOW:

·········Presents·········

Great Inspirational Romance at a Great Price!

Heartsong Presents books are inspirational romances in contemporary and historical settings, designed to give you an enjoyable, spirit-lifting reading experience. You can choose wonderfully written titles from some of today's best authors like Peggy Darty, Sally Laity, Tracie Peterson, Colleen L. Reece, Lauraine Snelling, and many others.

When ordering quantities less than twelve, above titles are $2.95 each.
Not all titles may be available at time of order.

Hearts♥ng Presents
Love Stories Are Rated G!

That's for godly, gratifying, and of course, great! If you love a thrilling love story, but don't appreciate the sordidness of some popular paperback romances, **Heartsong Presents** is for you. In fact, **Heartsong Presents** is the *only inspirational romance book club* featuring love stories where Christian faith is the primary ingredient in a marriage relationship.

Sign up today to receive your first set of four, never before published Christian romances. Send no money now; you will receive a bill with the first shipment. You may cancel at any time without obligation, and if you aren't completely satisfied with any selection, you may return the books for an immediate refund!

Imagine. . .four new romances every four weeks—two historical, two contemporary—with men and women like you who long to meet the one God has chosen as the love of their lives. . .all for the low price of $9.97 postpaid.

To join, simply complete the coupon below and mail to the address provided. **Heartsong Presents** romances are rated G for another reason: They'll arrive *Godspeed!*